On the Cover

The picture shown on the cover of this book
is the old Huff cotton farm dating back to
the 1800's. In the center is the barn that was
built by the family and that exists today
thanks to the care of the present owners who
have continued to preserve the history of the
land. The vantagepoint is the series of
ridges that extend south from Lookout
Mountain into northeastern Alabama. The
name of the nearest town is Slackland. The
area is known as Huff's Gap.

Acknowledgements

First to Val
Bethany
Jordan
Danielle
And
James

With special thanks to my
students

Preface

The Huff family that I call my own is both unique in its history and common in its path. The family migrated to Philadelphia from Hough, England in the 17th century. Little else is know of the lineage except that it had its origins in France. The original family name was De La Hough. Spelling changed for the purpose of ease as the relatives moved form place to place. From a position status in Pennsylvania, the family moved to Virginia to live the life of planters. The route then led to South Carolina where the family lived on the Saluda River near Greenville. The Huffs were planters of cotton there in the early part of the 19th century until South Carolina became "crowded" and the soil overused. William H. Huff, recently wed to Mary A. Hall, packed up and moved to the newly formed land of Alabama. The couple settled on a tract of land in the northeastern part of the state which was owned by the Cherokee Indian tribe and bordered by the Creeks. Stories about the Huffs and their interactions with the Indians are still told in this part of the state. One tale is of Cherokee Indians borrowing food from the family and leaving part of a deer on the doorstep of the house as payment.

The section of land where all these events took place over one-hundred and forty years ago became known as Huff's Gap in honor of its earliest white inhabitants. The land today is as it was then, being owned by only two other families since 1833. The Glens who are the present owners, are careful guardians of the history and spirit of the land, leaving it pristine so that one could almost picture the Huff veterans walking back to their beloved farm after a hard fought war. The family spring still pumps fresh, clean water. And the old barn still stands with the help of the inheritors of the property. My cousin, Patsy Abel, is responsible for the tracing of the proud history of our mutual Southern family, and it is because of her efforts that I was able to recreate this narrative based on fact. Although all of the events of this novel can not be verified, the conditions and situations represented are accurate based on the times. The characters are real. The places and names are also. The military reports are detailed based on actual documents. What you read of battles is likely what the actual characters saw and heard. Letters from soldiers in the 22nd Alabama support the narrative and help create a vivid picture of Civil War combat. The Huff family participants, their wounds, and service are authentic. The class distinctions are carefully recreated to establish a story that is believable. I hope you enjoy your journey to a far away time and place that was all at once beautiful, romantic and peculiar. Go back to the Old South when you read <u>For Love or Honor</u>.

Author's Note

It is my hope that African-Americans are not offended by the depictions of slavery in this novel. The events that are recorded are all based on fact. The preponderance of Southern literature reveals a very intimate relationship between whites and blacks in the War era. The record of abuses perpetrated on slaves is well documented in American literature and has become the generalized view of servitude. There is another story which is seldom portrayed, but represents the norm of relationships in the Ante-bellum South. I have been told by historians that what I am attempting to do is "a difficult thing". I wished to show an accurate picture of master, servant interactions without appearing to show slavery as a perfectly acceptable institution. To avoid doing so, I borrowed many stories from slave narratives and plantation documents, and wrote them into the novel. I was deeply moved on many occasions by the tender relations between the races, and looked with regret on the current situation we have found ourselves in. The majority of blacks and whites in the Civil War period rose above the title of master and slave that each inherited, and found a way to show their humanity. The unbreakable bond of master/servant should no more be forgotten than the atrocities suffered by the unfortunate slave. Few African-Americans can look back to the Old South with anything but anger and shame because of the legacy left by a biased history. African-Americans have a great deal to be proud of with respect to their role in the War Between the States. It is estimated that 65,000 to 90,000 blacks served the Southern army in every possible position. General Nathan Bedford Forrest had 30 black Confederate cavalryman serving in his elite forces. Ten percent of the 4th Virginia regiment was African-American. The list is too great to enumerate here. And the homefront! It was the wish of many planters that after the war a monument be erected to the dutiful servants who protected the places they considered home. It is unfortunate that the contribution of African-Americans who served the Confederacy are forgotten because of a skewed version of history that will not allow the image of a black supporter of his Southern homeland. Nor will it allow the image of a black soldier and a white soldier fighting side by side in a Confederate line of battle. It is the hope of this author that people of color will look with pride, at the character, the devotion, the loyalty with which many of their ancestors served their homeland. The fortunes of the races in the Old South were helplessly intertwined. They shared each other's losses; they celebrated their mutual joy. And so it is today. May our futures be so intertwined that we may rise above the racism which destroys the hope for a better America.

Chapter One

John woke to what he considered to be a new morning. It possessed a certain hope and promise that could not be attached to any other day in his recent memory. His life as of late had been hard, but since his return home mere existence had given way to real living. Days seemed to run together in Huff Gap, with the previous day looking like all the rest. The cycle of planting, harvesting, and delivering seemed endless. It was not a very exciting life before the war, and now that the shooting was over, it seemed even less so. But the last few days were hardly routine. There is a fullness, a depth which one wishes for his passing of time here, and although it is unrealistic to expect each day to usher in a flurry of new wonderment, a digression from routine would be as welcome as a farmer's rain. Those had been his thoughts until a few days ago. Although yesterday was definitely not routine, it was also not what he was wishing for. One must take the bad with the good, and much of yesterday was *very* good.

It was with this thought that John Calhoun Huff raised himself upright in his narrow bed of good southern pine, and poising himself on the edge of the soft down bedding attempted to reach both spindly arms heavenward. One did not respond. An abrupt sensation of pain accompanied the spontaneous movement. Being back home did not mean everything was the same as it had been. He had almost forgotten about the injury. He retracted his arm and planted both feet firmly on the cool plank floor, then let out a prolonged groan as if addressing the day itself in some ritualistic greeting. It was not without reason that this particular day, August 20th, 1865, was noted by John as a significant one in his burgeoning life. As in most significant days it was inexorably entwined with a day in the recent past. That day for John was yesterday.

The scattered small farms and rare plantation house spattered the hillsides and valleys of northeastern Alabama. John had seen any number of these familiar dwellings on his occasional wanderings, and they never ceased to stir in him a furious love for hearth and home. He was just returned from the war, and this was his first outing to beloved places. Although it was not his own beloved place, he had always held that he would never see a sight quite so wondorous as the Croft plantation house in Turkeytown . And as the road widened away from the thickness of trees, he was again upon it. The spacious home and sprawling grounds were an inspiration set along the two mile trek to the Coosa River. In his twenty-six years, he had made the familiar jaunt a multitude of times and each time he passed the stark white columns that rose like sentinels skyward, he slowed his wagon and turned his head westward like a soldier passing a review stand. It was a rare turning, for most often his piercing blue eyes were transfixed on the dusty, bumpy lane that lay ahead. As he gazed at the stately homestead, a splash of color emerged from the picture frame before him which was dominated by the hue of a white column house, blowing cotton, and billowing clouds. It was a swatch of pale lavender, and it was a dress. Attached to the dress was a sight that made him realize he had new things to learn about beauty. She was far more beautiful than the stately residence that reposed in the distance. John reined up the pair of anxious mules, and the jostling crate he was riding in lurched to an abrupt halt. At the disturbance, the maiden revealed herself to be quite young. She turned her face fully toward him and in the short expanse between them he could see her fine bronze skin, the color of which reminded him of mama's flapjacks. He was momentarily amused at the unlikely comparison, and doubted she would be very flattered if he shared the thought with her. His eyes lighted upon her full red lips as she parted them to speak.

---- Goodday sih', may I be of some assistance?

In his momentary reverie, he had forgotten that he had stopped for indeed no apparent reason, and he felt himself flush as he searched for the words that would satisfy her reasonable question and at the same time leave with her some noteworthy impression of himself. John spoke slowly and in jerks.

----No, ma'am, I guessed- maybe- it was you who was need of some help.

He winced at the conclusion of the last word wishing he could have thought of something else- anything else.

----Why, whateva' foa'? Is thea' some unseen peril hea' that I have in my naiveté' ova'looked?

The sharpness of her words and the directness of her gaze set him aback. She stood in full view now and John could only conclude that she was no less than exquisite. Her light brown hair was voluminous, and cascaded downward gathering in a heap of shimmering curls upon her delicate shoulders. A few renegade strands tucked beneath her chin and rested upon the lace of her dress. Her dark eyes were soft, but sharply focused. John gulped hard and began again, hoping to disarm her.

----Oh, no ma'am. I only meant, you ah' so fa' from the house , and this is a well traveled road and as you know the rabble from Owl's Hollow travel hea'. I most assuredly regret any insinuation...

A faint smile creased her lips- her eyes relaxed their sharp stare and traveled the height of his countenance. She was appraising him. He felt maybe he should open his mouth and let her examine his teeth as he did when looking over a horse he wished to buy. It was then he regarded himself. His hair was strewn and looked as dark and thick as chewed tobacco, and his slouch hat was perched on the back of his head. His clothes were blotched and his face streaked. He was in that moment very aware of the ridiculesness of not only his situation, but also of his appearance. Her eyes again rested upon his, and it appeared that either his words or his discomfort in fact put her at ease. It did not, however, permit him to relax when she again released her smile to respond.

----I am shua' a gentleman of yoa' quality would neva' bring dishona' to a lady oa' himself with such an offense.

He paused for a moment, unsure of her remarks. She was certainly quick-witted, and he couldn't decide if she were mocking him or exonerating him, especially given his appearance which did not suggest Southern genteelism. But there was something in her delivery that made him believe she was after all, sincere. The best thing to do he reasoned was to end quickly, gather himself, and return again another day.

----You speak my hea't, miss...

----Sophie

8

----Miss Sophie.

It was in an instant that the speaking of her name brought also the understanding of who she was. He knew he should have recognized her sooner, but the change in her was quite dramatic. He determined to have a little sport with her since she as yet had not reached his point of revelation. He spoke with pretended earnest.

----As I was about to say, yoa' obviously a woman of great strength and would requia' nothing in the way of protection oa' help af any kind from the likes of me. It is obvious that thea' is nothing that a man could do that you could not. In fact, I would waga' that you could fall off yoa' horse at full gallop ridin' past yoa' neighba's farm, and get yoa'self right back on with no help whatsoeva'.

She was stunned. The very recently brash but composed belle of the South stood with shoulders dropped, arms at her side and mouth agape in a most unladylike fashion. She then gasped, and her eyes brightened with her own recognition of the gaunt figure before her.

----God in heaven, is it you John?

The brightness in her quickly dimmed as she attempted to align the husk stepping down toward her with the strapping man she had known. The look was one of a certain sadness and regret thrown together with unabashed joy and fondness. He was aware of her mixed response and he understood it.

----I had told no one of that day. I had no idea how someone might know, and then I realized.

She moved hurriedly forward and he caught her in a firm embrace that betrayed his apparent frailty. To her further surprise, he picked her up and twirled her about just once and setting her down again amidst the sounds of laughter, held her at a long arms length. She could not help but notice that one arm was left immobile at his side.

----You were fifteen when I left. Look at you now. You have grown considerably in foa' yea's Sophie, and have become quite a lady. Yoa' father must be very proud.

----I've given him no reason to be otha'wise, but let's not talk of me. I have pressed yoa' fatha' and motha' often foa' some news, but they had heard very little.

He flashed a knowing smile through an etched face. He looked of a man who had seen too much sadness and had taken on its likeness, a bit like a pet that after a time begins to resemble its owner. It was not an overt sadness, but seemed to run much deeper than the shallow lines which marred his pleasant face. John released his hold on Sophie not realizing until that moment how tightly he must have been holding her. She could not have known how long it had been since he had held a women in his arms, and that he had never held one quite so splendid as she looked in that moment. The misplaced vision that assailed him momentarily, was of the pliant ten year old plowing through a field of yellow annise in profusion, chasing a monarch butterfly with no obvious intent except the pursuit itself. He could even remember her simple cotton dress, softer in blue than a robin's egg. As he watched her sidle slowly away, he was ever aware that she was no longer the little girl he left four years and a lifetime ago. She looked over her shoulder and beckoned him.

----Please, come and sit a spell. I would like to hea' what has befallen you these yea's past. That is of cou'se, if you can fo'give my abruptness at yoa' arrival. There have been a numba' of unwelcome suitors as of late.

Of that, John had no doubt. He wondered to himself if she had met a welcome suitor as of yet, but did not verbalize the thought, conscious that he would sound far too anxious to know this early in their reunion. She extended her hand to lead him and he took it in his noting the soft silkiness of her skin. Hardship of the kind he had known, evidently from the gentleness of Sophie's hands, had escaped the Crofts. He was glad of it.

He had almost forgotten where he had been going before the pleasant distraction, and his mind focused attention again to the wagon laden with bales of cotton resting on the roadside. He reluctantly dropped Sophie's warm hand and tended to securing the team to a nearby magnolia tree of ample girth. As he neared the tree blooming with white flowers, he breathed in deeply and caught the fresh lemony scent it offered. He was surprised to find it still in bloom this time of year. He had seen these trees all over the South and had never really appreciated their sweet fragrance until after his tenure with the army where soldiers bivouacked in camp were known to have fallen ill from "noxious fumes"- a stench so great that it caused illness. John breathed deeply again as he wrapped the reins around the dark gray bark of the young magnolia. He turned on his heels and with a few strides of his lanky limbs was again beside Sophie walking past the fields of ripened cotton. Two-score negroes plucked the white tufts from stalks, singing harmoniously as they worked. The melodic tones of "Jacob's Ladder" swept across the fields providing a rapturous air to the nature of things.

---- I don't but on occasion vencha' this fa' out to the fields, but I had to see foa' myself if oua' oversea' had ova'stepped his bounds. My se'vant Sadie tells me Jack has been beating the help with cowhide straps. Daddy has made it clea' that we will allow no such abuse. Since he is not hea', I saw to it myself. Jack is faithful but a bit zealous. He has ambition, but it clouds his judgement at times I fea'.

John marveled at her strength. She had been a tomboy for as long as he could remember. She had developed that spunk into a very self-assured woman of some independence. John had been amused by it when she was a child, and now he found it becoming. He had never been impressed with the ladies from town who were so bent on marrying a man from the "right" family they changed like the wind, depending on the traits the gentleman in question might require.Sophie would not likely comply with that approach. John responded with his own thoughts on dealing with the servants.

----Papa always held thea' was no reason to whip on the negros. They could find a thousand ways to pay back the beatin'. It's just back economics, not to mention shameful for good Christian folks. Northena's still see life down hea' like a page out of <u>Uncle Tom's Cabin.</u> Why, I only know one in the whole county who even beats his se'vants. You would think too that the Yankees would have to wonda' why they didn't rise up oa' leave when all the men folk were off fightin'. It is very disturbin'. You've seen that none of them have left since the Yankees liberated them. Had we beaten them as some do, I believe many would have gone by now.

----Yes, I know. Daddy has told them they ah' free to go. Some don't yet unda'stand. We carry on hea' knowing it could all change tomorrow. My dea' Sadie came to me the otha' day, nearly in hysterics sayin'," Miz Sophie, theyz tellin' me iz gotsta go livs someplace else. Iz donts hasta go now duz I? Youz my family Miz Sophie?" I told her she could stay as long as we still could eat, then we would all have to go. Then thea' ah' Quinton and Tobias who vowed to kill the Yankees if they laid a hand on me, the dea' ones. It seems oua' way of life hea' is soon to change, John.

He did not wish to think on that just now. She had in just a short time helped him pack away much of the despair that had ruled his daily life. Together with his coming home it seemed as if he might truly live again. Talk of an upheaval in his developing picture of the future would have to wait. He changed the subject as they entered a narrow alley shaded completely by neatly trimmed boxwood trees that reached a head taller than himself. They lined the lane on both sides for a hundred feet. The smell of them always reminded him of something very old and the trees helped to consecrate whatever they were near as aged and important. It was a cool passage to the main house. He saw as he turned his head to speak that Sophie walked very erect with her shoulders back and head high. She was graceful in every movement from the shifting of her clasped hands to the evenly spaced steps of her feet. He was unaccustomed to the pace. They emerged from the darkened tunnel into the blazing afternoon sun. They passed the gin-house which was normally stuffed nearly full with cotton bolls and the weigh station which was presently dormant, but soon to be bustling with activity. They stopped not far from the house and paused to rest beneath another even larger magnolia. Sophie sat on a poplar bench made for

13

two, and John stood waiting as a gentleman should for an invitation to be seated. He didn't have to wait long.

----Please, do sit hea' with me. I have much to tell you.

Before he could move, he was interrupted by the approach of a tall, middle-aged black man with head bowed slightly and eyes diverted. He held his wool cap in both his hands before him. His trousers were brown wool, tattered at the knees, and his shirt was muslin with pinstripes in goldenrod. His tight beard and hair were speckled with gray.

----" Beg your pa'don, sih," and turning to Sophie, "ma'am"

---- Go on Job. You know you don't have to be fo'mal with me. Gracious Job, you've been pa't of this family longa' than I have.

---- I know Miss Sophie, that's why I came to tell you pe'sonally.

---- Tell me what, Job.

A tear appeared on his weathered cheek, and he looked at her now directly with obvious discomfort. His words were clear and precise, and he spoke them in a low, deep voice.

---- Miss Sophie, yoa' daddy and mama have been good to me. I cants' complain. I'll neva' fo'get the pa'ty he threw for me and Tabby the night of oua' weddin', or the breakfasts we had at the house every Sunday. I especially thank you Miss Sophie for teachin' me how to read and write. But what I have to tell you is-I ha'ss to go. My brotha', he has got a fa'm in Mississippi and he wants me to come. And, well, I think I can get my own fa'm and all. I hope you will fo'give me.

Sophie looked on him with compassion. He had come to the farm in 1840, and she recalled him sharing

14

with her one night a desire to read. She determined to teach him and had done so late evenings on the piazza after his hours of toil. She spoke to him in a reassuring voice.

----Thea' is no need foa' fo'giveness, Job. We'll miss you hea', but we'll manage just fine. You ah' always welcome. God go with you, Job.

----And wiff' you, Miss Sophie.

Bowing slightly, he parted.

---- And so it begins, John. Very soon thea' will be otha's. We can not well manage this plantation alone if they all go.

Of this fact John was well aware. The Croft land adjacent to his own was a five-hundred acre farm. There were only eight such large operations in Cherokee county. They had nearly one-hundred servants compared to their own farm of one-hundred eighty acres, and no purchased help. John knew a lot about the workings of the county since his father, William, was a commissioner. He also knew most of the families would be unaffected by the loss of slave labor since of the 3,000 families in the county only five-hundred even had any servants, and most of those had fewer than five. The greater loss would be to those poor farmers who had sent sons to war never to return. This would constitute much of the South. So it was with keen awareness that John spoke.

---- You and I will see a new South, Sophie. It will be a life left to the me'cy of the conquera's. And if you have seen the trail of destruction that leads through Atlanta, you know that thea' will be little me'cy from the Yankees. I fea' we will be left with only oua'
dignity, and they will attempt to strip that from us also.

The conversation was getting far too somber and this time it was he who responsible for the tenor of it. He redirected after a few moments of awkward silence.

---- Ah, do you rememba' bein' down on the riva' the week befoa' we all left? It was a bright night and the reflection of the ha'vest moon rippled on the wata'. You and I, Warren and young George watched as the lights of the <u>Laura Moore</u> approached. We could see the steam rise from her stacks as the white smoke passed in front of the moon.

----I do rememba'! Warren lit a pine torch to signal the boat ashoa'. When it paddled oua' way we ran. I never laughed so ha'd- I was out of breath. I could hea' the captain hollerin' all the way up the road.

They both laughed with the warmth of the memory. John thought of Warren, his elder brother by a year, and George, just thirteen at the time. The two of them, close in age, had been very close. They both attended the newly formed public schools created in '54. Past memories brightened the pained faces.   The moment was fleeting.

Over the sounds of their laughter could be heard the faint report of a pistol. It was John who heard it for what it was, and being familiar with such sounds determined it came from the road where the team was tied. He called for Sophie to stay put while he raced back the path from which he had come. He passed through the boxwood alley, the fields of now chattering negroes, and was quickly upon the road and the wagon. The sight was a disturbing one. John walked over to a dark form lying beneath the fragrant magnolia. He was face down, a wool cap on his head. It was Job. In the distance a band of blue-clad raiders shouted and waved their hats before they disappeared in the dust. John kneeled over the fallen man and lifted him slightly. There was a dark red stain on the red clay dirt. His eyes were wide open and near his head a clenched fist that gripped a piece of crumpled paper. It was the letter from his brother that held the hope of his new life. John had seen men dead and he had seen them die, and he had become in a way almost numb to it. But this death began to gnaw. He had just seen the aging black man, and there was a radiance in him that could only be hope. Now, it was all spoiled. He could hear excited voices approaching . He determined quickly what he would do. With excruciating effort, he in an instant hoisted the cumbersome shell into the wagon. He unfolded the wool blanket he used as a seat cushion and draped it over the body, which when exposed revealed three wounds to the torso, one being in the heart. As he unreined the mules he saw Sophie making haste in his direction. With a loud "getty-up", John hurried away, shouting over his shoulder, " I'll be back"

He had already seen too much grief. His own he could manage, but he could not watch others mourn.

Chapter Two

As John made his way to the ever-winding Coosa, he contemplated the rashness of his decision. There were any number of problems that might result from his hasty flight from the Crofts, not least of which being what Sophie might be thinking right now. He had gone quickly enough and was at a distance that she could not have guessed what had happened. A gunshot along the road was common enough, especially at such a time as this, when it seemed the whole world had gone mad. More pressing was the issue of transporting a half-hidden corpse riddled with gunshot. In his periphery, John caught glimpse of a blur.

A brightly colored yellowhammer bolted from the cover of a nearby chestnut tree fluttering cheerfully as it passed. Its pleasant song and vibrant color were a strange contrast to the pall that enshrouded the silent passenger. The creaking wagon moved slowly along, laboring beneath the weight of its cargo. To his left, John spied a large spot of purple wildflowers that he recognized to be heal-all. An idea formed in his head as he looked on the serenity of the spot, and having something of an analytical mind he thought on the simple irony of it. He would bury Job in the heal-all. It was known to cure any number of ailments from loss of blood to colic. Just maybe it would serve as balm for a troubled soul. John again brought the useful beasts to a stop, and he pulled the tools he carried in the event of a wagon emergency from the back. He meandered a short distance into the field and began to dig. As he dug the morbid hole in the heavenly earth, he recalled the night he had dug a hole near the family smokehouse in October of 1861.

John had gone to Montgomery with his father on county business. At the capitol building they had passed Representative Starks. John had listened intently as the distinguished statesman repeated what the politician had told Congress with regard to secession. He emphatically insisted that if the slaves were emancipated and he was left poor he could well live with it; he had been poor before. His greatest objection was that the bounty of Southern production was being diverted in the form of taxes to build the infrastructure of Northern industry. He referred to the South as the "milch cow" of the North. And with respect to the slavery issue, he believed emancipation as the North would have it, would displace an entire race the likes of which history had never known, even in the Biblical exodus, and would turn Southerners into immoral people who would have to kill to defend. For northerners' seeming lack of reasoning, he doubted slavery was the central issue. He was certain the Yankees would invade.

And John purposed to defend. He told papa at one quiet time during the one-hundred and fifty mile trek home that he wished to enlist. The family patriarch did not respond. His jaw was set and his eyes narrowed. John had spoken it with alacrity and had expected a word of praise from his father. Instead he nodded and spoke no more of it for the remainder of the trip. When there was a call to arms for the men of Cherokee county, he and Warren, already members of the local home guard, decided they would set off for nearby Centre the next day to join cotton broker Colonel Deas of the newly formed 22nd Alabama regiment. George had overheard the conversation and although normally quite reserved, declared boisterously his full intention to go along. Warren told him he could not go being only thirteen, but George had prevailed, swearing he'd go one way or the other. He would not be separated from his two older brothers.

Mama had grown ashen to hear the news and her expression changed little through the merriment of the sending off the following evening. There was a bonfire, peach brandy, but mostly neighbors and friends gathered to send off their sons of the South for the pride of Alabama. The pig was roasted and stuffed and exuded an aroma to be remembered on days of near starvation. The most poignant moment of the evening occurred when Warren stood in the glow of the dancing fire in the close embrace of Julia, his betrothed. She did not want him to go. The words could not be forgotten.

----Please, stay hea' with me and we'll move up into the mountains.

----Dear Julia, the way I see it, one can fight foa' love oa' one can fight foa' honor. It is foa' yoa' love that I live. For honor I may well die. I do not see how I can possibly have them both. I can not stay and be the man you could love.

The words were oppressive and made liquid clear the reality of war. All dreams of glory and heroism were in that moment set aside for a brief glimpse of what was likely to be the bitter truth. It was a truth that most of the wide-eyed soldiers could not fathom. The War might end their lives. When the evening had ended, the brothers had stood huddled together. Each held an object in his hand, wrapped and covered. Warren instructed them all to place the package into a tin which he then placed a lid over. It had been his idea to choose a prized possession for the sake of remembrance to place in a hidden spot. Whichever of them survived the fight to come would unearth the tin and carefully guard the contents within as family keepsakes- a lasting memory. It was an eerie compact on a cool fall night. John had dug the hole near the corner of the smokehouse. It was this memory that returned to him.

Returning to the matter at hand, he finished the grave and was satisfied with its depth. He then threw off the cloak that had hidden Job and grabbed him by the muslin shirt, bringing him to the ground. The body was extremely heavy. Regretfully, he dragged what remained of the man to his final resting spot which John decided was as good a one as a man could want. The owner of the land was an elderly man and the spot would not be disturbed for some time. He pulled Job through the violet flowers of heal-all. As the soft pedals were crushed beneath his feet and the weight of his traveling companion, they released their delightful perfume. A perfect picture of forgiveness he thought. You trample a flower and it offers up its sweetness. Maybe there was something to this heal-all after all. John positioned Job in the narrow hole and folded his arms neatly. He then placed the wool blanket over him and shrouded the body. He stood over the depression with bowed head, sweat dripping from his nose, and examined his work. He felt a few words were appropriate.

----I stand hea' to speak foa' yoa' se'vant Job.

The words sounded contrived. Was he God's servant or the Croft's?

He would think on that later. He continued solemnly.

----I didn't know him well, but believe him to have been a good man. May like the Job of old he find returned to him wealth and happiness. May his mansion be splendid and his soil eva' fertile.

And he added.

----May throngs of angels ha'vest his fields.

He was pleased with the words and he hoped that Job could find the forgiveness which would truly allow him to enjoy God's blessing, if one is given that opportunity in heaven. But John decided it would not be an easy thing to forgive those that had taken so much. And he wondered for what purpose they had taken the man's life. Or if he could forgive those who had taken so much of his own. Without further ceremony he began to fill the lifeless void in the Alabama dirt. When the deed was thus finished, John turned his attention to other matters. He retraced his steps through the heal-all, leaving the fresh mound behind. As he again mounted the wagon, he thought on the myriad of complications a hasty decision could bring on. It was like that climactic moment in the heat of battle when a choice is made between going forward, staying or fleeing. Each has serious, even deadly consequences, and yet the decision must be made instantly. Then you live with the choice or you die with it, either way you would often choose the other if the opportunity would arise again. John moved the boxy transport closer to the river. He remembered he told Sophie he would be back. He didn't say when. He didn't feel he could face her just now, especially knowing there was this deception between them. He could still see her fine featured face blazoned in his memory and he knew when he became an old man he would be able to conjure it up. And it would make him smile. Or maybe, even better, he would turn in his bed and see a clearer image. Her ever present image. He was a little surprised at the endearing thought. He wondered for a moment where the transition from sweet neighbor girl to potential mate had happened. And what about his obvious concern for what Sophie might think of his appearance or his actions. His most recent thoughts before returning home had been for his own survival, allowing little room for the feelings of others. One thing for certain, she already seemed to be occupying a great deal of his idle moments. John was thinking on the significance of these things as he passed a grove of Magnum Bonum apple trees. The aroma was mood altering. These rich yellow apples with deep red stripes were a favorite for baking pies. John looked on the multitude of ripened fruit and could picture a dozen pies set on a half dozen window sills, a gentle breeze blowing the sweet smell into the upper living quarters, permeating every corner with its cheer.

The vision brought to his memory his walk to Centre to join the regiment where he had last seen the fruit. With his two brothers on either side, they had moved at a hearty clip down the five mile road to the county seat. Their cheeks were ruddy and their steps were light. They had laughed and jostled each other for a few miles when by good fortune they happened upon a tree of Bonums. They had stopped and pulled a score of them, shoving all but one into their shoulder sacks. Had he known what would later come, he would have spent them all more slowly, like shiny new coins.

John had not noticed a large divot in the lane before him, and the wagon leaned into the crevice. The change of balance caused the weight to shift and the distracted driver was jolted back to the road that lay ahead. John saw a fair distance away, dust was kicking up, and a rider was approaching. It was a singular dark figure on a dazzling black horse that was nearing at a rapid pace. He could make out his black suit and hat, and his shirt was blindingly white. The solitary rider neared to a hundred feet and John could see a smile expand on his ebony face. Obadiah Means, a free black farmer of reputation pulled alongside as his glistening steed snorted hot air through flared nostrils.

----John Huff, praise be! It sho' is good to see you. We thought you was among the dead.

----So did I foa' a while, Obadiah. It looks like you've passed the time well.

----Could be betta' if they'd continue the railroad on up to Chattanooga. Yo' daddy's wo'ked ha'd on it. It'd save us a lot of money passin' through oua' prope'ties and all like it would. It shur' 'nuf won't happen now.

----That's ok, papa has anotha' plan. You hea' he applied foa' a distillery license?

----Oh my, yes. From a planta' to a cooka' of whiskey. What has this war done to us?

----Made us moa' resourceful I suppose.

----Maybe I'll take to making National flags foa' the new guv'ament. They ah' in large demand I hea'.

----They'll need moa' by the time we burn all of 'em they've tried to hang ova' Alabama.

----Just like yo' daddy- a fighta' 'till the end. So long , John

----Bye now, Obadiah. Be watchful. Thea' ah' a lot of raida's on the road.

He had always liked Obadiah. The man had worked as a slave and was given his release when his owner died and willed him free leaving him a sum to start his own farm. He had done well with what he was given. When it came time for the war, he signed on with Nathan Forrest and rode with his cavalry. There were about thirty other black soldiers in that cavalry unit with him. He was injured early in the war and came home. John knew what most of the yankees never would --that about 75,000 negroes had fought side by side with white folks in the Confederate army serving in every capacity. He had talked with a few prisoners who were greatly confused at seeing so many blacks supporting the Southern hord. It was just one of the many misunderstandings between them.

Obadiah was very articulate and had a good business sense. He had even purchased some servants of his own. John thought it a curious thing to see the poor servant humbly standing before Obadiah receiving a severe tongue lashing at the hands of his smartly dressed black owner. Whenever the freeman came to visit, he was amiable, full of conversation, and generally entertaining. John respected him fully. There were about forty such free blacks in the county and John knew many of them. Most had worked very hard and had prospered when the economy was at its height before the war. They too were now suffering from its ravages.

John came to a point where the road bent around a hill covered with mountain laurel. Rounding the curve, the path opened up to reveal a panoramic view of the Coosa River valley, stretched out before him in a hot, late summer haze. The sight was breathtaking, and he never ceased to tire of its beauty. Down below was

Croft's ferry and the activity of planters on the wharf, and steamship workers busying themselves on the decks of the "Coosa", the first boat of its kind to navigate these waters. It was nestled close to the shore and John moved his cargo into the valley to fulfill his days' mission.

Chapter Three

Sophie returned to the house with some amount of agitation brought on by her puzzlement at the strange events and by her powerlessness to change any part of them. Her conversation with John had been a pleasant distraction, and seeing him, despite his hollowed appearance was somehow comforting. Given all he had endured and survived she somehow felt safe when she was close to him. He exuded a certain strength which was evident in his speech and in the durability of his body which had weathered an immense amount of abuse of a nature she could only imagine. Whatever he lacked in handsome appearance he certainly made up for in pure male virility. Not that he was much lacking in attractiveness. It occurred to Sophie just then that she had noticed little else of John than those vibrant blue eyes and inviting smile, and it brought a smile to her own face. She wished him back. Sophie entered the door under the ornate fantail perched over the entrance and between the coach lights set on either side. The expansive parlor with polished oak floor and towering ceilings opened before her. She rushed past the serpentine backed sofa lined in red velvet and up the white stairs. The vast array of windows allowed an explosion of sunlight to pour into the open room illuminating its deep reds and clean whites. The sight reminded Sophie of a strawberry patch on a cloudless day. The windows allowed more sunlight than usual, the curtains long ago being used for clothing during the recent troubles. Although Cherokee county suffered less than most of the South, especially Georgia and South Carolina, Union raiders had passed through and had done some amount of damage. The Crofts had lost hogs, horses, chickens, most of the vegetables they had grown for their own sustenance, as well as candles, clothes, horseshoes, wagon wheels and other useful items including cooking utensils. They were fortunate to have hidden their horses and carriage along with some silver they gave to the servants to bury. But there had been little use for resistance. The shouting exultant blue troops swept in quickly and descended on the farm like a plague of locusts. Sophie had stood at the top of the stairs and berated the intruders very indignantly. She did manage to discourage a few young privates who attempted to pass by her to gain access to the upper living quarters. She had balled her fists and proceeded to pummel the fair faced boy who reached her first. He looked little more than a child. He howled when a well placed kick sent him reeling back the way he had come, and in the process sent the second soldier tumbling down the stairs in a more rapid descent. She momentarily wondered where the real soldiers were, and in the ensuing calm moment she discovered. The more hardened veteran soldiers had obviously found the servants. From the sounds of their cries and the laughter of the oppressors she determined what must be happening to them. As she hurried to the back of the house she saw what she wished she had not seen. The amoral tormentors were availing themselves at the expense of the slave girls who stood helplessly by, weeping uncontrollably and calling on God or some sympathetic soldier to help them. Their pleas went unheeded. *And so these are the liberators*, she thought. *God help us then* . The remaining negroes screamed and shouted and ran about in a very excited fashion. Papa sat in a high-backed chair in the parlor with his head in his hands. It was a pitiable sight. Aunt Molly, the faithful mammy, had gathered up ten year old Louisa and the other two girls and they were huddled together in the outdoor kitchen figuring the house would be burned. As fortune would have it the Yankees were in a hurry and left the house and fields bare but unmolested otherwise. One scowling, unkempt Billy Yank inquired in a tone loud enough for all to hear if they should burn the house. The reply came back, "We'll save the burnin' for Mobile." And they left as quickly as they came.

Sophie passed the spot on the stairs where the soldier suffered indignity at her hands. She moved swiftly down the hallway and into her own chamber. The room was painted in cheery yellows and rich golds. A pretentious Chinese rug woven in a tapestry of gold, black and nutmeg centered the room, upon which rested in part a walnut canopied bed topped in white lace. Sophie proceeded to the wash basin and splashed her dusty face with the refreshing spring water. She caught a glimpse of her visage in the mirror and was sorry she had. It was shameful for a lady of the status she was to be, to have such darkened skin. Her milky white skin was battered by the harsh sun. One would think in times such as these that some laws of refinement might be relaxed, yet knowing the ladies of town she doubted that she would be exempt from their biting comments. The tanned face would have to be rendered in the order of things rather insignificant. Papa had been ill and there were no brothers to see to the business of the farm so a

29

great deal had fallen on Sophie. She had endured the hardships with strength and grace.

Sophie turned away from what she thought to be a very unforgiving mirror and threw herself with a sigh on her goose down bed. She began to fancy the days events. Seeing John was certainly the pinnacle of her day. She smiled as she thought on the carefree days of her early teens. She had been charmed by John for as long as she could remember, but given her age and his, she recognized a relationship was not likely to happen. The years that transpired since they last spoke profoundly changed her life, his, and the world as they both new it. The chaos that reined along the roads was just such an example. Gunshots, thievery, pillaging were now commonplace, where once there was order and serenity. Still something troubled Sophie about the scene out front earlier. John had left so quickly. Surely he wasn't in pursuit of someone in that rickety wagon. It was all very curious. Well, there would be answers soon enough.

----Sophie, may I come in?

It was Louisa and she sounded very low.

----Why of cou'se. Come in Wheezy. What's troubling you?

Louisa entered and sat abruptly and with some force at Sophie's feet. She hesitated to speak, but then turned up one side of her mouth and asked,

----Do you think I'm pretty?

----Oh Wheezy, who could possibly question it? Why with yoa' auburn hair and fai' skin, the boys must be beside themselves in yoa' presence.

----Well, thea' is only one I'm concerned about, and he doesn't seem to notice me at all.

----You probably make him anxious. And besides, at thirteen shouldn't you be conce'ned with moa' than just one boy? Who is he, if I may ask?

----Oh, I can tell you Sophie. *He* is William Huff.

----The son of Mista' William Hardaway Huff, our neighba'? Well, what about that?

----Please don't say anything to Papa. I know he likes the Huffs, but you know how particula' he is about us marrying into a propa' family.

----I well know Wheezy, but talk of marriage is a bit prematua' now isn't it? Anyway, I'll say nothing. I think the gentleman William would be a very fine choice. He is very fortunate to have yoa' affections. He just may not realize it yet.

----Thanks Sophie. I knew I could talk to you.

Sophie could hear the familiar shuffle of the Croft's butler, Quinton. Quinton had served the family well. He was quite refined and highly intelligent. He was chosen for the job by Papa for his ability to learn the English language quickly, and his eagerness to please. Guests always conveyed their highest praise for Quinton and he always beamed when the words greeted his ears. Most of the other servants were quite jealous of him, his finer accommodations and his intimacy with the family. The shuffling stopped just outside her door.

----Miss Sophie, Masta' Pratt has called on you and requests yo' presence in the pa'lor. Do you wish fo' me to give him an ans'a?

----Thank you, Quinton. Tell Mista Pratt I will be with him presently.

Louisa interjected.

----Speakin' of good choices, Sophie.

Louisa smiled and excused herself, followed by Sophie who was walking and brushing the wrinkles from her dress. As she thanked Quinton and passed out into the corridor, she could hear rising up from below, the resonant sounds of the family piano. Stephen Pratt stopped playing and stood as Sophie descended the stairs. He glided to where she was and bowing slightly, offered his hand. Her gaze met his and she accepted the gesture. He was flawlessly dressed in a pair of brown tweed trousers, ivory vest, high collared white shirt and sweeping black hat. His hair was as dark as his black shoes so that his head, feet and knotted cravat were perfectly matched. He broached the silence with a liquid voice.

----My dear Sophie, you look positively radiant. My father sends his regards. I apologize for the delay in visiting, but there was business in Montgomery that was pressing.

----Stephen, you know thea' is no need for apology. If you must attend to matta's of business, I will simply have to manage alone, as unsavory as that may be.

Stephen smirked at her reply. He was by now used to her acrid sarcasm. He was well aware that she would prefer solitude to his company, but for the life of him he could not understand her apathy toward him. Was he not the most sought after bachelor in Montgomery? He decided he would play along as he walked her to the parlor.

----So, how are the plans going for the wedding?

----My fatha's wishes for a wedding do not guarantee the fruition of one. I think you ah' being a bit too presumptuous. Why, you have not yet asked foa' my hand, and you certainly do not yet have my heart.

----Ah, the heart is the greater matter.   Maybe I shall have your hand first.

----My hand you may get.

----Easy Sophie.   I was only playing. You must have heard our fathers talking of our union when you were in town last month.   They seem very excited by the prospect.   I fear they will press forward with their wishes.

      And Sophie feared it also.   When she told John she had done nothing to make her father anything but proud she had this very situation in mind.   She had not told her father she had no interest in Stephen, chiefly because he had been ill and she did not want to disappoint him.   Her marriage to a Pratt would insure financial stability for the family through whatever hard times were likely to fall on the plantation.   The Pratts were the founders of a business that created and maintained cotton gins and their parts in Montgomery. Having no sons and failing health, her father counted on her interest in Stephen.   But there was something beyond the gentlemanly ease of Stephen that unsettled her. To nearly everyone else he seemed ideal, and he lacked for nothing in material wealth or in the interest of the ladies. Sophie, however was not enamored by him.   She found him both arrogant and superficial.   She hid her feelings from her father very well.   She couldn't figure Stephen out.   She had always thought men to be rather simple creatures, but the actions of this one confused her. Stephen neither protested their evident merging, nor did he pursue her vigorously.   But really, why should he be concerned that he did not love her?   He would dress her finely, parade her about town, and expect her to bear his children.   If it was passion he wanted he would call to his chamber one of the slave girls, thus filling his life with all that he needed. What do men know of love anyway? No, he would not protest.

The thought caused Sophie's face to contort, and seeing she was agitated, Stephen attempted to break her thoughts.

----I was just on my way to the Glens to see about the possibility of supplying them with a new gin. Will you walk with me to the road?

Sophie and Stephen talked casually avoiding any talk of nuptials as they trod along the same path taken earlier by John and her. When they came to the road that bore the Croft family name, she bade Stephen a polite good-bye and searched the lonely road for some sign of movement. And she wondered where John might be right now.

Chapter Four

The crowd was much smaller at the ferry than what was usual for the time of year The year's crop failure was in large part to blame as well as the desolation of the recently ended war. One of John's only childhood memories was that of his trips to the river with his dad and brother. Before the steamship "Coosa" starting running the Coosa River the cotton crop had to be moved down by flatboat to Montgomery . The 400 lb. bales would be hoisted by pulley onto flatbed carts back at the farm and hauled by mule to the ferry at Croft Plantation. Pa would load the bales on the flatboats made of lodgepoll pines and together with Warren they would ride the sometimes treacherous Coosa down the river to Wetumpka where the cotton would be delivered to the factor. The families' factor in Wetumpka, J. M. Bradford, was charged with the selling of it, as was the custom, and usually Mr. Bradford sold to his connections that sent the cotton on to Mobile where larger ships bound for Europe would deliver it the textile mills. Since steamships started navigating the Coosa in 1845 goods could be shipped upriver to Rome, Georgia. This permitted access to Atlanta, Chattanooga, Charleston, and the North. John could also remember the maiden voyage of the "Coosa". He stood along the shores of the river with a throng of others as the small white boat chugged its way up from Double Springs, which later had been renamed Gadsden. The motley assemblage cheered and hooted as the steamboat fired its single cannon as was customary for the maiden trip. It was indeed a momentous occasion.

John eased the wagon around a rather severe bend and into an open spot near the water. The crude steamboat rested near enough the landing that some rather wide planks stretched from land to boat providing access. John had suggested to Mr. Bradford a price of 12 cents a pound, a favorable rate for his cargo. He was willing, however, to leave the selling to his factor who had been very good at peddling the family cotton at the most advantageous time. The profit margin was still, however, very low when expenses for storage and toll were added, as well as insurance for the safe delivery.

John was watching a pair of muscular negroes unload the wagon when he heard someone call his name. He turned and saw the man's proffered hand before he saw his face.

----John Huff, I heard you was back. Lordy, I thought you was kilt fer shua'. Thea' was a John C. Huff of the 22nd that was killed at Shiloh, and we just fig'red it was you. Who could have guessed thea' was two of y'uns.

John smiled broadly as he pumped the hand of James Sewell, a neighboring farmer to the south of his own family's farm. His boys joined up with the 28th Alabama regiment because an uncle was put in command of it, and neither one of the lads had come back. John was wondering if the man's exuberance was some tragic distortion of his own boys' deaths and that he imagined mistaken identity was the reason for his sons' absence. That maybe seeing him here gave the man some false kind of hope. More likely, James was just that glad to see him alive. He had not yet let go of John's hand but was shaking le ss vigorously now.

----No, I was only shot. The otha' John got captu'ed by the Yankees and taken to Camp Douglas, which I guess is about the same as presumed dead from what I unda'stand of that prison camp. I was close to dead at Chicamauga, but that neva' got back to anyone I hea'. Just as well I guess.

John felt uncomfortable talking about his near misses to a man who had the misfortune of having none. He could read the response in the other's averted face before it came.

----Well, you prob'ly heard I lost Matthew and Charles.

The obvious pain was there. He would not soon be over it. More grieving---there was just no avoiding it. John in that moment wanted to go hide in the mountains, live off the land, stay away from the hurting , suffering, dying people. But no, that wouldn't do. Everything dies.

----Yes, I heard James. They were fine boys.

He thought about saying something about dying for a good cause, but the words would sound hollow, the cause being only a fading memory already having lost its ability to stir or comfort. The struggling man nodded then remembered.

----I was sorry to hea' about Warren.

John thought briefly about his happy, outgoing brother and accepted the condolence. Whenever someone said Warren's name it gave John a bit of a jolt. Sometimes it was hard to remember that he was no longer around. It was easier to pretend that he was still off somewhere and would return in a few days. James changed the subject.

----How did yoa' crop fai' this yea', John?

Next to death of kin this year's harvest was second on the list of most depressing topics. To James however, even crop failure was a pleasant distraction.

----Neva' had a wo'se yea'. But we're betta' off than most. Pa took some measures last yea' that saved us. He took only the best seed from the last crop- was real ca'eful about it. Little things like that made a big difference.

----Glad to hea' it. Hey, we're havin' a gatherin' tonight at oua' place if you haven't heard. Shua' love to have ya'.

Before there was an opportunity to respond, a crushing explosion rippled the air and the ground tremored in unison. The "Coosa" lay before them, the focus of a great deal of commotion. Her deck was ablaze and splintered fragments of rail littered the water. Men were cursing, crying, calling for help. A boiler had blown on the ship and chaos reigned. Seeing the desperation of two scalded men not fifty feet in the water before him, John sprinted to the landing, leaped into the river and quickly reached the first floundering man. In his desperation, the struggling victim grasped and clawed John as he neared, jeopardizing the safety of both of them. Had John the use of both arms the task would not have been difficult. As it was, he labored. John tried to calm him but the shock of his plight and the burning skin caused him to panic. In his desperate attempt to buoy himself the striving man grappled with his rescuer, and John plunged beneath the surface. He felt the water engulf him, and a foot on the top of his head. He quickly became disoriented, and by the time he began again to rise to the light, a hand found his shoulder and forced him back down. No matter how hard he struggled to surface, he was again and again thwarted in his attempts. His lungs began to ache as he flailed about; His body was beginning to fail him of exhaustion. In a desperate effort he forced himself through the tanglement of writhing human limbs and broached the surface. He focused quickly on the thrashing man before him and with a weary left arm, his only good working one, landed a still powerful jab to the jaw of his unwitting assailant. He began to sink . John quickly recovered him and dragged him to shore, struggling with every stroke. Several bystanders rushed to his aid and began attending to the near lifeless body on the wet ground. The fire on the "Coosa" was quickly extinguished due to a Herculean effort and John could see it still smodering as he passed through the onlookers. He hauled his own bedraggled body to the wagon. He with effort got in the seat and looked back at the scene. James was at the shore attending to the other of the two victims. John waved in his direction and turned the wagon back to return home once more.

As he traveled back the dusty road John thought how curious it was that he nearly lost his life trying to save a man. He had spent the last four trying to kill them, and he had managed to survive. How ironic it would have been to lose his life in the effort to save a stranger. He wondered who the man was he had just rescued. Did he have a family? Would he ever wonder who it was that spared him? John recalled the recent disaster of the Sultana. The steamship was carrying former Union prisoners when the boiler blew up. The vessel was grossly overcrowded and seventeen hundred people sank into a mirky grave.

Well, now there is one less victim to be offered up to the gods of sea. He'll probably want to know why I socked him. Anyway it sure felt better salvaging a life than taking one---or burying one, he thought to himself. He passed the place where Job now lay, a shrine to the rules of fate. John turned his attention back to the forward road and where it inevitably must lead. Sophie. He hadn't yet determined how to handle the situation. He told her he would be back, so he must stop. But he had not yet decided if he would reveal to her what had happened on the road earlier. No, that would have to wait. He would not lie to her. So what could he say that would be truthful yet evasive. Sounded like an excercise in splitting hairs. Or debating how many angels could fit on the end of a pin. There was a job that he had to do that had just occurred to him, so he figured to tend to it immediately. Yes, that was the truth.

Voices from behind him startled John from his pensive state. A group of about ten negroes materialized out of the woods and onto the trail. Was this the band of killers John had caught sight of earlier? John dismissed the thought. Although the emancipated slaves glutted the roads, they were rarely a threat to anyone. Most tested their freedom by talking a "trip"---a pleasure not afforded to many of them during enslavement. There were those however that were quite disgruntled having believed they would be given lands after the war. Instead the conquerors were instituting their own version of slavery by making former slaves sign contracts and returning them to the plantations they had previously worked on. There was the realization that little land would be divvied out. Most, however, chose to stay with the families they considered their own, and in most cases it was fortunate they did. Emancipation had brought a very dark, uncertain, and hostile world. So if these were of the former mind, trouble may well be afoot. The ragged band of black males passed near the wagon. John spied his Enfield rifle resting on the floor beneath his feet. He was very glad that he had buried it before the surrender. He had foresight enough to realize it might be useful in civilian life when the whole mess had ended. He could get it quickly enough if necessary. One who appeared to be the leader spoke as he passed.

----Well, lookee at massah now. He is all wash up. What, you gotta do a nigga's work now?

Another chided

----Lookin' like massah is out in da field all alone and wif'out his whip.

John reached under his seat and pulled out the long Enfield. It had claimed many lives with a deadly accuracy that John had spent years attaining in the hills around the farm. The leader spoke again, throwing a look over his shoulder as he passed the slow moving wagon

----Pullin' a gun on niggas---I wonder what da Bureau would haf to say 'bout dat?

They all broke out into a derisive laughter before they went their way. They seemed to enjoy their new ability to be insolent after the years of repression. But as was most often the case they turned out not to be a threat. The threat of the Freedman's Bureau however was a real one. Although there were only twenty of their officers in the state, the possibility always existed of being arrested for some injustice against the former slaves and hauled in for questioning before the magistrate on the complaint of a negroe. And before he new it he was nearly upon the Croft plantation home again where this day had begun to get strange. The band of freedmen left the road as quickly as they had appeared and made their way across open fields. Up ahead there was much dust that could only indicate another sizable party of individuals probably on horseback. The cloud drifted above the path that led to Sophie's manor house and out from its midst came a high shrill scream that was distinctly female. John wondered what else could possibly happen this day. Then remembering the marauders, John rushed to the area of the smoking road. He raised his rifle to the sky and sounded a warning shot to fend off whoever may be there. When the squealing mules arrived to the scene, John jumped down to where Sophie was picking herself up from the ground. From the sound trailing off down the road, it appeared that the rogues had returned for more sport. But why here? It didn't take much speculation to deduce that the attack on Job and the one here on Sophie were not random acts. It appeared he arrived before she had taken too much harm, or at least he hoped. She shed not one tear but her voice trembled as she spoke, in spite of her obvious determination to appear unbothered by the assault.

----It would seem I do owe you an apology. It certainly is dangerous out hea' on the road. Thankfully, you appea'ed when you did. I don't know what they would have done next.

She stood before him a wilted flower. Her hair was tousled, face and dress dusty, the latter torn at the shoulder revealing an obscure patch of smooth white skin that was quite in contrast to the dark, dusty face to which he with concerted effort returned his attention. John believed she somehow looked even more attractive than when he had seen her earlier in the day. He asked her the obvious question.

----Did they hurt you, Sophie?

----No, they knocked me down and held me fast. They wanted to sca'e me and they succeeded in that. From the wild look in thea' eyes I believe they were certainly capable of committing the worst of crimes.

And then she broke down. She put her hands to her face and began to cry constrained, stifled sobs. John moved toward her to comfort her but was suddenly startled by a rushing rider on a dapple gray horse. He arrived with amazing swiftness on the scene. He was wearing brown tweed breeches and he carried his black hat in his hand. He leaped from his horse and dashing passed John, enveloped Sophie in his arms. She returned a half-hearted embrace. Stephen cupped her face as he spoke.

----Are you all right Sophie? I heard a gunshot and came as quickly as I could.

He stood back and examined her, being sure she was unharmed.

----Yes, Stephen, I am fine thanks to John hea' who fia'd the shot you heard.

Stephen turned and flashed a row of perfect white teeth set against sleek black hair. He addressed the stranger with words that were carefully formed and purposeful.

----Well then, John, I owe you a great debt for saving my fiancee'.

Fiancee'? The words struck John hard. He had felt like this only twice in his memory. The first was at Shiloh when he had taken a minnie ball to the chest. The ache he felt now was very similar. He received Stephen's extended hand as Sophie attended to the rules of decorum and introduced Stephen.

----John, I would like you to meet Stephen Pratt. Oua' families have been friends foa' yea's. He is up today from Montgomery.

Her voice was quiet. Her manner subdued. She now spoke to Stephen directly.

----John Huff has a fa'm very close to hea'. We played togetha' as children. He is recently returned from the war quite a celebrated soldieh'.

Stephen's smile, which he could display when needed, quickly faded. It was a source of contention with Sophie that he had avoided service in the Confederacy. And he had suffered more than a little ridicule for it over the past years. He looked at Sophie trying to determine if the comment was made innocently or if it was an intended dig because he errantly used the word fiancee' a bit prematurely. There seemed little doubt as his questioning look met her sober face. He turned again to John.

----Well, Sophie and I are grateful for your safe return.

John replied in earnest.

----I consida' it a privelage to assist a lady, especially when she is also a friend.

John's face scrunched as a thought occurred to him about what had just happened there on the road. He redirected a comment to Stephen.

----You must have passed the outlaws on the road eitha' comin' or goin'.

Stephen shook his head.

----No, that road was as blank as a picked field.

John shot a glance down the barren road that led to his own home. It was all very odd. They were surely headed for Owl's Hollow, that holdout for deserters and thieves.

He questioned Sophie.

----What did they want, Sophie?

----They said that we were being offe'd a fair price foa' the plantation and we ought to take it if we wanted to live. They said to take the money and leave hea' oa' thea' would be anotha' death. Papa just sent word yeste'day that he was well and would be home next week. I do not know what they could mean. Everyone else is accounted foa'.

John had not counted on this. He did not want to tell her now, and not this way. But he had no choice. He bowed his head to avoid her eyes, then looked to her again as he spoke the words he wished not to speak.

----Sophie, earlia' today when I came out to the road I saw a man lyin' face down. I didn't want to tell you.

Her saddened eyes pierced him through, but she spoke not a word. He could see very clearly the hurt and disappointment There was no need for her to tell him what she felt. She turned, and before he could explain further, she walked slowly back to the house. John wanted desperately to go to her, but he could not will his limbs to move or his mouth to speak. Instead it was again Stephen who followed her to the house and out of sight. John could do nothing but mount the wagon and return home. He thought hard about the day. He thought about the death of Job, the man he saved from drowning, the engagement of Sophie and the threat that the attackers delivered to her. The Croft plantation was certainly a fine property, but many such plantations were failing all over Alabama and being sold at depressed prices. Why did someone want *this* property? John turned onto the wooded lane that ended at his home. He guided the wagon into the short tunnel that bore into the slight rise in landscape, and passing out the other side he could see the expanse of fields before him. The house and barn sat in the apex of a pie shaped tract of land set between Red Ore Mountain and Shinbone Ridge, which was the tail end of Lookout Mountain. To John it was a comforting sight. In roaming from Kentucky to Georgia during the war, the memory of this place kept him at peace, and gave him the hope that he might one day return here to live out his days. On two occasions when very near death it was just this vision that he knew would be his last. He moved the wagon up near the old salt box construction house that featured a loft and sloping roof. On either side sat two giant black walnut trees that John loved to climb as a child. A twisted path wound to the spring that carried the cleanest, clearest water anyone had ever had. Just beyond the spring house lay the barn and chicken coup. The backdrop for the buildings was a mountain green with trees and dotted with white round spheres of hydrangea. Death Shade Hollow formed at the point behind the house, filling with an eerie mist on warm moist mornings. Dawn here in Huff's Gap smelled clean and fresh with walks in the hills bringing the heavenly scent of ginger crushed beneath plodding feet.

From atop the ridge the only blight on the pristine valley was the house and barn below, and off in the distance one could see the winding Coosa, the connection to the rest of the known world. Here was his haven, his joy, his life. And it occurred to him he had no one to share it all with, and even that was a strange thought since he was here with ten other brothers and sisters and his folks. Still, it wasn't the same. It was a beautiful place to share, and yet like an evil twin just a short distance up the road, there was Owl's Hollow that held many secrets and a great deal of danger to outsiders.

Chapter Five

Morning broke clear and bright on the Croft Plantation. Streams of light like butterscotch burst through the boxwood alley and cast golden rays in sporadic beams into the tunnel. Sophie could see the spectacle from her window, and it seemed to lighten her load that she thought too much to bear the night before. Stephen had followed her to the house and she sent him away with a flourish. She retired to her room and wept the night away, allowing the palpable darkness to sweep her further into despondency. A new day can bring some amount of healing, but even such a glorious morning is no panacea. And Sophie was troubled. It was hard to say what troubled her the most. The threat loomed large in her mind. There were so many questions that she was sure her papa could answer upon his return. And there was Job. The thought of the soft spoken man for whom she had such heartfelt affection saddened her deeply. And John had deceived her. Why didn't he tell her what had happened? Did she appear so fragile that he thought he must protect her? She had fought off a Union invasion of her home, organized contracts with the former slaves to secure their continued labor, and tended to her sisters and ailing father, all without his help. And Stephen. Why did she care so little for him? Sophie decided she mustn't cower in the house all day. No, she would go out today for a ride. She stepped outside her door and called to Quinton.

----Quinton?

----Yezzum.

----Could you have the carriage prepa'ed? I am going foa' a ride.

There was a silence, then a shuffling, and Quinton appeared midway up the stairs.

----Miz Sophie, afta' what happened yes'rday I had hoped you would not be movin' about 'till yo' daddy came home. If he knew I let you back out on da' road, he might be findin' me a new place to live.

----Thank you foa' yoa' concern Quinton, but I'll not be made a prisona' in my home, noa' will I be intimidated by a band of rabble. If they wanted to ha'm me they would have done so yeste'day. You can tell Papa that I insisted in spite of yoa' urging. I'm shua' he will not question the accuracy of that.

----Yes mam, Miz Sophie, but I must say you do trouble me sometimes.

----I'm sorry Quinton. It seems I trouble everyone.

Quinton smiled faintly and removed to do her bidding. She freshened her swarthy face, pinned her hair up and descended the stairs to the waiting carriage. Tobias, the driver, was a dark man in a dark suit. He was sitting in a black carriage behind two ebony horses. The horses, carriage, and rider were like an ominous dark cloud just outside the door. It made for an eerie scene on a luminous day.

----'Tis a God-kissed mo'nin', ma'am. Whea' do you wish to go this fine day?

Next to Quinton, Tobias was the most envied of the servants. His position as driver was a good one to hold. He could travel about, meet and talk to others, and avoid the hard labor endured by the "hands" as they were often called. He was quite proud of his favored status and boasted of it often to the others. Since emancipation and the transition to contract work, Tobias had not once disrespected his mistress, mostly because of his abiding regard for her. He had seen her labor to keep the plantation afloat, and her generosity to the servants was well known. He was quite fond of her.

----Take me to Leesburg, Tobias. We ah' lacking in some necessities that I can secua' thea'.

Tobias seemed pleased by the choice. He smiled, and after seeing Sophie safely aboard, pressed the team to embark. The black procession moved passed the white fields which were slowly being stripped clear by the field hands. Sophies efforts to establish contract work had not been completely successful. Many of the workers, it was apparent by the lack of numbers in the fields, had just refused to start work this morning. They were establishing their own terms for rendering service. Sophie was powerless to do anything about it. Under the old system, work began at sunrise and continued after dark. Only a short break was given during the course of the day, and each hand was expected to achieve an adequate weight of cotton by the time that work day was done. On many plantations, a shortage of output meant a flogging, which was why every servant approached the gin house with a bit of fear. Too much weight meant an expectation for similar results the next day. Too little and a beating was to follow. The end of a work day always brought anxiety. Papa, however, instituted a system of incentives. Overages in production went to the servants to encourage hard work. Beatings were avoided except in extreme instances, and things went smoothly for the Crofts. The same incentives were offered to others such as the blacksmith who purchased his own freedom with what he earned from his labor. Papa was proud of his approach as a business man and as a Christian. Some had even adopted his policies. Still, as was evident here, working the cotton crop was extremely distasteful to many of the former slaves. Sophie was not surprised. It was a constant reminder of their servitude. She tried to impress upon them the advantage of staying with her, citing the limited options available to freedmen. For most it had worked, but she still could not control their labor even with incentives. A fair number still expected government intervention that would grant them large tracts of land of their own, and they were simply biding time until their share was given.

They were past the fields and onto Croft Ferry Road that had been the scene of so much commotion yesterday. Sophie shuddered as they moved jerkily out onto the thoroughfare. They moved westward with the sun at their backs, and all the while Sophie searched the way ahead for some sign of five outlaws whose visages she could recall with perfect clarity. Tobias guided the carriage north toward Leesburg passing scores of travelers of every class, merchants, freedmen, farmers, speculators, and the like, conducting business as usual. This year had brought a whirlwind of commerce to north Alabama. The desire to resume business after the conflict was at the root of the zealousness. Many were making a lot of money, while many more were losing everything. Sophie hoped she would not be among the casualties of an economic war, more for the sake of her father and sisters than her own. She felt that she herself could well bear it, if all was lost. Sophie could not endure seeing her proud father laboring to survive in his weakened condition. As unpalatable as Stephen was to her, their marriage would fix a myriad of troubles. To hold out for love would be not only foolish but selfish as well. If she were in fact in love she might feel differently. But she wasn't. In fact she wasn't sure she would recognize it if she was. She didn't believe men knew what love was, and yet neither did she. And maybe she would never know. Sophie rolled her eyes and puffed out air from her bottom lip so that the strands of hair that had escaped, fled her forehead. It was also a sign of her exasperation with the whole notion of love and romance.

----You warm Miss Sophie?

Tobias' question was less out of concern than it was -a not very subtle remark- about her layers of fashionable yet foolish clothing. Her dress was elegant but not garish. It was checked in crimson and blue with corset, hoop, vest and other assorted accouterments layered one upon the other. Her face was glazed with a mixture of baking soda and flower to make her seem more pallid than bronzed. Beads of perspiration began to streak the concoction revealing the tanned skin beneath. She was obviously uncomfortable, but there was not much of a choice when venturing into town other than to look presentable. A wry smile broke on Sophie's smudged face.

----Tobias, you ah' fo'tunate to have been granted freedom. As long as we women must wea' such restricting garb, we shall foa'eva' be bound. And I do mean bound.

Sophie reached both hands to her waist to adjust the constricting corset which added to her discomfort. She twisted and turned until she attained some measure of relief.

Tobias laughed heartily and guided the carriage into town. Leesburg wasn't much of a town, but there were a few good merchants conducting business. Tobias stopped abruptly at Ross Supply, a dealer in gifts and trinkets. Sophie had decided that in spite of her anger with John it would be discourteous not to thank him for his aid at the time of her assault She would put her feelings aside to purchase a token of appreciation that would only be appropriate. She knew just the thing. She spied on a shelf nearby a small leather bifold that opened up into an oval which, although blank, held a place for a photograph. She looked at the empty oval and wondered what picture he might place there. She hadn't heard mention of any love interest in his life. Maybe it wouldn't be such a good gift after all. Surely, though, there must be someone's image he would wish to keep close to him. Yes, it would do. Sophie was well pleased with herself that in spite of how furious she had been with John, she was still able to do what was right for a lady to do. Giving him the token might be a more difficult matter, though.

Sophie turned her attention to finding something to place at Job's grave, if in fact there was a grave. She had just assumed John had buried him somewhere on the way to the river. What if he just dumped him somewhere in the woods and left him to the scavengers? What if he rolled him in the river. One who has seen the horrors of war may have lost all sense of the dignity of man. She had heard the stories of men who were left dead and dying on the field of battle when there was no possible way to retrieve them. Why would he even *bother* to bury a slave? She became concerned, and angry with John all over again for his deceit. She looked again at the leather frame, considered placing it back, but took it instead to render payment. When she turned, Sophie was startled to find she had bumped into someone now standing directly in front of her. The girl was rather plain, dressed in homespun of a drab, earthy color. She looked to be Sophie's age. Her face and smile were nevertheless pleasant, her voice being as slight as her frame might suggest. She looked vaguely familiar.

----Sophrenia Croft?

The girl spoke with obvious deference.

----Yes, foa'give me, I'm ce'tain I should know you.

----Oh, it's quite all right. It's Susan. Susan Huff. I'm John's oldest sista'.

----Why of cou'se, Susan. I haven't seen you in some time. How ah' you?

The contrast between two women of the same age could not be greater. Sophie stood in her finery, the picture of a Southern belle. Her waist, already small, aided with the corset looked no bigger than a sapling. Her impressive dress bloomed to full size at the floor. Conversely, Susan wore her ragged garment she normally reserved for home. It was course and lacking color, not something one would typically be seen in with exception to work. Susan, though backward, seemed at ease even though she was very aware of the ostensible difference between them.

----Considerin' the harsh times we ah' fairing very well. Losing Warren was of cou'se very difficult foa' us all, but we remain thankful to God that John and George have returned to us. Though they ah' not completely well they ah' at least alive and foa' that we ah' grateful. You ah' fo'tunate you had to send no brotha's to thea' untimely deaths.

54

It was not an intended slight. It was a comment one might say to another who had contributed little to the "cause", suggesting his or her sacrifice was minimal. Susan had only wished to convey her loss and her regret that any should so suffer. Sophie saw the concerned look as Susan began to explain her words. She understood, and reassured the apologetic Susan.

----I would that I had brotha's to give. Not one retu'ned home to me. I suppose you also had twice my joy having two brotha's come home. Instead, I mourn foa' many friends. I count Warren as one of them.

----Thank You Sophie, I had almost foa'gotten how well you knew Warren. He talked often of how you made him laugh. Why John was saying just today that he had seen you, and he said too how splendid you looked. Oh, he told stories of you, and he, and Warren when we were all younga'. It seems so long ago.

Sophie missed Susan's last words. She was gnawing on the part about John having taken notice of her. She hadn't thought he much cared how she looked. Splendid, he said?

Sophie reentered the dialogue as if she had missed nothing.

----Oh my yes, we did have some fun.

----Speaking of fun Sophie, I'm hea' today gatherin' a few things foa' an evenin' at the Sewels. I know the family would love to see you. Would you come as my guest? Thea' will be dancing and good food. You know John has been very low lately. He would benefit most of all by yoa' company.

Sophie had always been a spirited girl, and she had run with the Huff's in spite of the class distinctions impressed upon her by her family. With such an invitation to spend an evening in the company of a soldier who needed her, she could hardly refuse. Besides, she wished to demonstrate, unequivocally, her disregard for wealth as a variable for friendship. Sophie accepted graciously to attend as if invited by the Queen herself.

----I would be delighted to attend, Susan.

----Wonde'ful then. I will see you at 8:00.

Sophie paid for the gift and hurried out to where Tobias was waiting.

----Were you successful, ma'am?

----At getting myself in a situation? Yes, I was.

----If I may ask ma'am, how did ya' do that?

----Oh, it's a complicated matta' Tobias. I ran into an old friend yeste'day who thought I needed his help even though he had no good reason to believe so. I was a little angry that he assumed I was so helpless. We talked a while and my anger subsided. I actually began to feel a bit of fondness foa' him and then he left abruptly which greatly confused me. He retu'ned and rescued me from an awful group of villains, foa' which I felt indebted to him.

----So you did need him?

----Well, yes.

----So that made you angry?

----Of cou'se not.

----'S'cuse me Miss Sophie, but di'nt you say he made you angry when he ast' if you needed help?

----Yes, Tobias, aren't you listening?

----Yezzum

----So anyway, I was grateful. Then he told me what he had done, all in the guise of protecting me, which I will sha'e with you soon, and then I was very hurt and furious with him.

----Fo' protecting you, ma'am?

----No, foa' thinking he needed to protect me.

----Yes ma'am, it sounds very confusin'. But whateva' he done, I'z sho' Massa' Huff meant well.

----Now, how did you know I was speaking of Mista' Huff , Tobias?

----Oh, deez t'ings git 'round Miss Sophie.

----Am I the subject of gossip now, Tobias?

----Yezzum

----And is thea' talk of Stephen and me?

----Oh, yes ma'am. Lots a' 'dat.

----Really?

----Oh, yes ma'am, they says that Massa' Stephen is about as slippery as a sow in a mudslide.

----They say that, do they? I assume *they* do not approve of oua' cou'tship then?

----No, ma'am

Sophie had her doubts about Stephen, but really had no foundation for feeling the way she did. It was of interest to her that others saw in him what she had felt as intuition all along. She should learn to trust it more often. The revelation did little to change things, however. The situation with the plantation remained the same. Tobias's insights, if he shared the ones he uttered, only served to make her more uneasy about the possibility of marriage to Stephen.

The ride home seemed much shorter, and before she knew it Sophie was back home and passing through the ornate front door. The brightness of the reds in the parlor were diminished in the pall of afternoon. The hues were more ominous, and instead of ripened strawberries, the room took on the impression of what Sophie believed a war hospital should look like with blood-stained walls. She could hear from a distant room the sounds of unsubdued laughter. They were her two youngest sisters, five and seven years old respectively, Catherine and Sally. Sophie's mother and theirs had died two years previously of a fever, and the children had laughed very little since. Their mammy, Molly, who had suckled them as infants assumed complete care of them both. Sophie would have gladly shouldered the responsibility had she not been consumed with the affairs of the plantation. She made her way to the open room and from the inside she recognized a resonant male voice. It was her father. Her step lightened as she rushed into the room with her arms open wide. He turned to embrace her and spoke in a gravelly voice.

----My Sophie

----Papa, I was worried about you. How ah' you feelin'?

----Tolerable my dea'.

Sophie's intuition was screaming. This time she paused to listen remembering what she had told herself earlier about trusting her instincts more. Through her father's shadow of a smile she sensed his trip had not brought expected results.

----Something is wrong, isn't it?

----No my dea', I feel well.

----But you've brought bad news.

His loose fitting face drooped into a frown. He would not skirt the inevitable. There was no more laughter and all stood listening for what they knew would not be good news.

----No one will advance us the money we need to plant anotha' yea'.

----But what of the five hundred bales you shipped to the interia' foa' safe keeping?

----It was all confiscated oa' stolen as gove'ment cotton. Oua' debts to the facta' ah' eno'mous and without the ability to clea' it, no one will advance to us, even though money from the North is flowin' heavily on the speculation of next yea's crop. You know it would be dishonorable to default on oua' payment to Ayers and Sons. They have dealt fai'ly with us foa' thirty years.

The old man paused and his expression turned quizzical.

---- Strangely enough I was offe'd a good price foa' the prope'ty by a man who came to the doa' one day. Sophie, we may have to accept his offa'.

----You can't mean it! A ca'pet bagga' fatha'? I will not allow those vulcha' damn Yankees to steal oua' home. What about the Pratts? They will help.

----We cannot ask friends foa' handouts, Sophie. I do still have some pride. The ca'pet bagga' knows oua' taxes ah' ova' due and he will take this place from us very soon. Even knowin' that will not turn me into a begga'.

----When Stephen and I marry the Pratts will assume the debt and foa'ward to us the capital we need. We'll borrow against the future crop as we have always done, just ova' a longa' term.

----Ah' you announcin' yoa' engagement, Sophie?

----Well, no, not officially.

----You ah' a treazha', Sophie. I am very proud of you.

The approval of her father meant very much to her, and so the words filled her up for one sustained moment. Then Sophie remembered the ultimatum delivered by the cold-eyed messenger with whiskey on his breath. "You've been offered a fair price". She guessed that the man Papa met by chance was not an accident. Apparently he was unaware of the aggressiveness with which they pursued the land. The attackers were using her to get the deal consummated. She doubted they had the means or the intelligence to carry out such an elaborate plan. Someone else was behind it. She new that Ayers and Sons was pressuring cotton growers to remit payment for debts accrued because they themselves were suffering from a lack of cash flow due to war conditions. Desperate times bring about desperate solutions. The sale of the plantation would mean immediate cash for the factor house. She resolved for one to get to the bottom of it, and for another not to alarm her father with the details. Meanwhile she would think on some other possible way of saving their home which she had no intention of giving up. As she excused herself from the room, the mood again became light. Papa had continued the games and beyond the laughter Sophie could hear her father cough and then gag spasmodically. In spite of his denial, she knew he was not well. Out a back window ghostly forms were moving in the closing darkness. The field hands were nearing the end of the days' labors. A face appeared distinctly and abruptly in the frame and then vanished. The man was unmistakingly Jack, the overseer. Sophie thought he was acting very queerly. And she had too, the distinct feeling she was being watched.

All of the frenzied jubilation was accompanied by the marshal music of military bands. The entire city was all aflutter with giddy expectations of quick and glorious victory. George recited the words of Colonel Zachariah Deas which could not be forgotten. "We are fighting for the cause of liberty just like our founding fathers, and no Christian man can turn away from his country's call," he shouted. John nodded as he too recalled the event.

And they remembered Warren on that day, uncharacteristically the more serious one, enlisting not for the excitement or dreams of glory, but for the honor of doing one's duty. So proud they all were, from Cherokee county, designated company D, 22nd Alabama Volunteer infantry. The one-hundred best that Cherokee county could muster. Company D was to be their family now. The last pleasant memory that George related was the glorious image of the 22nd, marching in parade fashion through the streets of the city. All supplied by their brave Colonel Deas at his own expense.

But then the mood shifted and George began the slow inevitable procession that led to a horriffic day in September. He recalled the hours and hours of drill, the aching body and the sore blistered feet. In an effort to return to pleasant thoughts, he talked of the camraderie of the campfire and his introduction to tobacco and "pop skull". There was an intermingling of all types of humanity. George talked of new-found vices that the older soldiers were more than happy to involve him in, enjoying the corruption of his youth and innocence. Those early days were more than a young boy's most adventerous dreams come true. They recounted together the day Warren was elected to be an officer. He was a natural leader and everyone recognized it. He was a man one could trust. A man of his word. He was kind and gracious, but a staunch believer in the duty of doing things the right way. They were proud to be called his brothers.

George halted and then pressed ahead with courage. He talked aloud the pictures that played in vivid color beyond the door. He started with the sounds of marching and a hundred tin cups clanging against canteens and "couters". He described the steam rising from the necks of the men's wool shell jackets, and the distinctive odor of that same filthy, wet wool mixed with sweat. And finally, George was to the deepest recesses of the hidden room behind the door. The battle began with the formation of lines.

And so he began to spill it out in a great flood. All the details and events that had led to his brothers death.

----The brigadia' shouted out, "Attention Brigade", and then the Colonel, "Attention Battalion", followed by the Captain's "Attention company". I knew it was oua' tu'n. Elbow to elbow we were, like packed sa'dines. You rememba', John.

And then the reason for the closed door.

----We began to load knowin' when we fia'd that we would be in Hell itself. We began to move and the ground was quakin'. Men we'h knockin' me off balance as they lost thea' footing. My mouth was very dry and my finga's were slidin' along my rifle as I moved to right shoulder shift on command. Ah gawd, the noise John. Do you rememba'? I thought that the noise itself was gonna' kill me---shake my insides out. Men were screamin', lookin' at each otha' with no sound comin' out. We were called to move oua' rifles to shoulda a'ms once again, and with it came the orda' to halt. It was like a million ho'nets were loosed upon us with the sole pu'pose of takin' oua' sanity. All I could hea' was a bzzz bzzz bzzz, and a thump, thump, and screams, lots a' screams---some high pitched, some gutteral. Cannon sta'ted belchin' deadly rounds a' solid shot and canistah'. That canistah' musta' been made in the devil's own wo'kshop. Hundreds a' little balls of shrapnel was rippen' flesh from bone and dismemberin' everythin' in its path. Thea' was blood, pieces a' bone, matted hai' all ova' me. The command came to fia', and then load. Thea' was chunks a' flesh and blood I tried to wipe from my face befoa' I opened my mouth to tea' open my ca'tridge.

George was speaking in monotone, squinting his eyes away from the scene, still looking at the dirt. He halted for only a moment and then continued on.

----I spilled the powda' down the hot barrel, and pulled out my ramma'. My finga's was slippin' when I heard the orda', "fo'ward march". I fumbled into my cap pouch, half-cocked my hamma', flicked off the ole' cap and put on the new one.

The whole while I was movin' and I sta'ted steppin' ova' writhin' masses of flesh. Thea' was a'ms, legs, hands, feet, and otha' pa'ts I could not even tell what they were. Thea' was the godawfullest smell a' blood, feces and urine. Thea' was some poa' souls with eye sockets gone, jaws gone with only a hole between thea' nose and neck. The whole ground was squirmin' like maggots in a pile.

George paused, remembering why they were there. His mind flashed to another picture.

---- You rememba', on the night of Septemba 19th we were camped in the woods along Chickamauga Creek. You had already retired but the rest of us slept on oua' elbows in readiness for General Longstreet's orda' to move. We were all pretty anxious, knowing what was likely to happen come mornin', but Warren was excitable. We were on the edge of a woodline about 6-800 ya'ds east a' Lafayette Road. He laughed, chatted, moved about regularly, lightening the tension among the boys everywhea' he went. I think he knew his fate, John, and he was okay with it. He kneeled beside me at one point in the night and said,

----Hey George, you take care tomorrow, and don't do anything foolish. Don't go grabbin' the col'uhs or such. You know mama would never foa'give me if I let somethin' happen to you. Don't be the first to run, but just as surely, don't be the last if it comes to that. You'll be just fine. And George, if somethin' should happen to me, not that I'm lookin' foa' it, tell Julia if I can't love her in this life- I'll love her in the next.

----He smiled that wide smile of his and looked into my eyes in a way that scared me. It was a long last look, John, and it haunts me still. But that's the way I like to rememba' him- smilin', with his eyes flashin'. Anyways, I didn't see him again until you and I formed in battle lines. I felt some at ease havin' you on my right as my file partna'. Warren looked at his time piece and I saw him whispa' to himself, "9:45", like the time had some meanin'. He smiled at me again and then moved to his place as file cloza'.

John then spoke up for the first time as his picture came into focus.

----I rememba' crossin' the road and engagin' the yankees nea' a place called the Vineyard house and driven' 'em to the next farm, George. We drove 'em to what they call now widow Glenn's house and that's when all hell broke lose. Ole' Willie Payne who was r'at in front of me took a ball to the head. I was tryin' to wipe his brain outta' my eyes when I found a Yankee bullet with my chest. I felt two thumps and fell to the ground.

----I felt ya' go brotha'. I'm sorreh' that I could'nt stop to help. You knew that didn't ya'?

----Soldieh's gotta' do his duty, George. Besides, Warren came to check on me. He stooped down, opened my coat and said, "Johnny, yoa' too aw'nry to die." He squeezed my hand, yellin' for a strecha' beara' and off he went.

----Just afta' you went down we moved past that fa'm house and the orda' came to move by the right flank. So we right faced and double-quicked until we hooked up with anotha' brigade. As we fronted and dressed I noticed that company E was lookin' mighty thin. They had some heavy losses that day. Five standa'd beara's were killed carryin' oua' col'uhs that day.Well, anyway we moved fo'ward about seventy-five yards and thats when we saw them yankees up on top a' steep hill they call Snodgrass. The Colone l, wantin' to take that hill yelled, "All right boys, let's show them yankees Alabama steel." A shout went up and we advanced. It was deadly. We was almost to the top and that's when I saw Warren. He turned and looked at me with his s'owad straight in the ai'. Then he turned to the Yankees and lowered it. We followed him to the top and that's when he went down. He was jerked upright with sev'ral shots all at once. When the Yankees had broke into the mist I went back to whea' he was. John, they tore his beautiful body all apa't. He was still alive but he was coughin' up so much blood I couldn't hea' him speak. He got a sca'ed look on his face and tea's were runnin' down his cheeks. He grabbed my sleeve and pulled me close, but he passed out befoa' I could get nea'. Stretcha' boys came and took him. I got word from Marrietta two weeks lata' that he was gone.

And it was all out. He seemed relieved that he would have to recount it no more. He had told the story, and as painful as it was to recall, he felt good with the knowledge that he had honored the memory and bravery of his oldest brother. A hero. But the strain of it was on his face, and it was clear that he did not wish to relive the ordeal again anytime soon. When he was able again to utter words, he filled in a few other details of the 22nd Alabama that had fought so proudly that day. The unit had been decimated. They had begun in Alabama with 1,000 men, and of the 371 men who entered the fray that day, five standard bearers were lost and 175 men. John was disturbed to hear it. He lost many friends that fight. The consolation was that it had been in routing the enemy. The fact that the cause was now a lost one dulled some of the luster of the memorable victory. The thoughts of Warren prodded the curiosity of the brothers, and they again focused attention on the disturbed place in the dirt that held the contents of their planning some years before.

----Should we just leave it, John?

----We made a pact George. I aim to dig up that tin and find out what Warren left for posterity. We owe it to him to finish the agreement.

So John began again to dig. He wondered if his whole life might be one prolonged dig with a few moments of meaningful life experiences in between. He had dug furrows for crops, holes for graves, holes to sleep in. He was rather tired of digging in the dirt.

In a short time he was upon the tin, and he reached to lift it out. It had faired well, he noted, and he brushed it off with a weathered hand. John removed the decorative lid and placed it on the ground. He reached for the carefully wrapped possession of George's and returned it to him. He then took his own and placed it in the pocket of his trousers. John and George both stared hard at the small package that remained. It was compact enough to fit in the palm of the hand, neatly wrapped in white cloth, tied with twine into a bow. John carefully unfurled the bow and unfolded each corner of the soft cloth. The first glimpse revealed the token to be of a shiny black and was of a sturdy composition. Another fold and it became clear to John he was holding an arrowhead. He smiled, sniffled, wiped his nose. But it was George who spoke, a little confused.

----It's an arrowhead. And a broken one at that. We have dozens of them here on the farm.

----Ah, but this one is special. You probably don't rememba' because you were only foa', but Warren and I were out plowin' the fields one afternoon when he called me ova'. You and Dilsey came ova' to see what he had found. It was an arrowhead in the shape of a heart. It was split almost in two. As he held the token high in his hand, he proclaimed in a loud voice with a seriousness which amused the onlookers, that when he found his girl he would give her half, and he would keep the otha'.

John clutched the keepsake in his hand and closed his eyes to relish in the pleasant memory. George again broke the momentary silence.

----So whea' do you think the otha' half is, John?

John was surprised he hadn't put it together yet, and he paused to let his slower witted young brother to catch up. After sufficient time John answered.

----I'm shua' Julia keeps it very close to her.

The two turned and walked quietly back to the old homestead. Susan and Edna had their noses pressed to the window as the boys neared, and from inside could be heard the boundless exuberance of the carefree youth. Six more children under the age of fifteen, Mariah, George's twin sister and the two eldest now at the windows. Eleven children in all, counting himself, though not a child, packed like cotton in a gin house along with parents William and Mary. His father, William Hardaway Huff, dearly loved to retell the story of how he found this land back in 1833 and had persuaded some good folks of South Carolina to make it their home. Susan saw them coming and greeted John at the door.

----I hope you don't mind, John, but I saw Sophie in Leesburg today and invited her to the Sewell's tonight.

The fact that Susan would even ask him indicated he must have sounded interested in Sophie. John didn't realize he had intimated any interest

----Why would I mind, Susan?

She smiled a sweat closed-lipped smile and turned to walk back inside.

----I didn't think you would.

George followed Susan inside still looking a little shaken, and John paused to think for a moment on the words Warren had spoken the night before they left for deeds of glory. "One can fight for love or one can fight for honor. I do not think I can have them both." And in his hand John carried the sentimental symbol of one that would live only in the memories of his family, and in the broken heart of the one he was forbidden by fate to have.

Chapter Seven

Sophie had hurriedly gotten ready for her evening at the Sewells. She did not want to appear pretentious so she dressed down considerably in a calico dress that would be appropriate for the evening. The two mile jaunt to the Sewells was covered in a very short time. The night was filled with sound and Sophie could hear the distinct echoes of familiar events. The servants' hounds bayed wildly in the distance. A favorite pastime for them after their labors were complete was the 'coon or possum hunt. Raccoon was hunted for sport, whereas possum was hunted for the roast. It was a very content negroe who had treed a possum and soon had him roasting over an open fire. From the sounds of these hounds a meal was as good as on the table. Even nearer were the sounds of the fiddles squealing their joyous tunes. Sophie could almost see the lustrous, happy faces of the African musicians as they moved rhythmically to the intoxicating music. She so completely enjoyed the festivity of a ball and dance. This barbecue would be somewhat different, she guessed. The feel of dirt beneath her feet would be quite a contrast to the great halls and homes she had danced the night away in. The dresses of course would be far less extravagant, and the company a bit more course, but many of the dances would be familiar. One thing was certain. It would be quite fun. *Southerners know how to enjoy life*, she mused, *no matter the social caste*.

She took from her handbag the gift which she had brought for John. She tried to rehearse how she might give it to him. Each attempt felt awkward. She decided to leave it to spontaneity. Tobias steered the wagon around the last curve of the serpentine path that led to the Sewell's. Sophie could see the focus of the festivity. A pig was skewered and roasting over a dancing flame. The aroma was heavenly. Silhouettes were outlined in the glow of the fire. One she thought she recognized. She stepped down and could see that it was in fact John. He was standing and talking to a group of men. They were listening closely to him speak. He had not seen her, thankfully, so her searching eyes sought out Susan. A gathering of young ladies were chatting near the shelter, and Sophie quickly moved to join them. Susan rose to greet her.

----Sophie, I'm so glad you could come.

----My gracious, Susan, the whole Yankee a'my couldn't have kept me from a dance.

Susan introduced Sophie to the ladies present, all of them being her senior by a few years, or so it seemed. They of course knew her if only by reputation, and being of the class she was, Sophie was received rather warily. Her manner was so charming however, that they warmed to her quickly even if it seemed they would rather have not. When the formalities were finished, the seven women resumed their conversation which, not surprisingly, was focused on the gentlemen present. It was young Betsy Sewell who reestablished the direction of their discussion.

----Oh, now whea' were we? My goodness how could I eva' foa'get? Susan, we were just discussin' yoa' brotha'.

Sophie felt herself flush. She hoped no one was able to notice. Betsy went on.

----I hope you don't mind the discussion in yoa' presence, Susan, but that brotha' of yoa's is divine.

----It's quite all right, Betsy. I'm getting ratha' used to it by now. I ashua' you John is very uncomfortable with all the fuss made about him lately. He is very shy and a pictcha' of Christian humility. I am of cou'se very proud of him too, as is all of Alabama.

The small circle opened to the fire to behold the object of their admiration. John was there, his back to them and smiling broadly as the others appeared to be having some good natured fun at his expense. They were throwing their heads back and patting him on the shoulder as they shook with laughter. A delicate young woman from Tennessee asked what was on the minds of most of the ladies present, if not all of them.

----And so you say, Susan, that he has no girl?

----Well thea' is one that I believe he admia's, but i'm not shua' she knows it, oa' that he would even admit to it, but he is, I can ashua' you, very available.

Susan shot a glance at a startled Sophie who quickly changed the subject for fear that she might be mentioned by name. Susan only laughed pleasantly as Sophie shifted the attention of the group.

----The food smells so delicious I'm not shua' whetha' I might eat oa' dance fi'st.

They all chuckled as Betsy said,

----Why choose? I'm shua' *these* gentleman would not be particula' if you were to do both at once.

Sophie had adroitly diverted the unwanted attention and turned in time to catch a wink and mischievous smile from Susan. She blew out a sigh and returned a half-smile of her own that acknowledged she had indeed gotten the message. The fiddlers struck up

74

"Rose of Alabamy" and the ladies dispersed to various partners and friends. Sophie was now standing somewhat alone and was beginning to feel uncomfortable, when a male figure approached rapidly toward her through the darkness.

----Sophie, I'm so glad I found you.

----Stephen! What ah' you doin' hea'?

----Now is that any way to greet your betrothed, Sophie?

----I am in no mood to play this game with you, Stephen. I demand to know why you have come hea' tonight, and don't tell me you were invited. You ah' spyin' on me.

----Not at all, dear. Please don't be rash. When I arrived at your home they said you had gone in this direction, and given the recent trouble I thought you might need some assistance. I am only concerned for your safety.

----Yoa' conce'n for me is no moa' than you might have foa' one of yoa' prized hounds oa' horses. If you were truly concerned you might have thought about whetha' oa' not I wanted you hea' tonight, instead of indulging yoa' own curiosity oa' God forbid protecting yoa' personel propa'ty.

----You are even more beautiful when you are angry, but truthfully I would prefer you a little less beautiful and a little more even.

His calmness at such times was maddening. The angrier she got the more levity he exhibited. It was as if he treated her indignance as some spoiled fit rather than a legitimate complaint. Again, as she had done before, Sophie turned and walked away. She did not know where it was she was going, only that she needed to be away form Stephen. As she hastened past the fire she heard her name called in a soft, low voice.

----Sophie?

She turned in the direction of the sound still not seeing who it was.

----Susan told me you would be hea'. Could we talk?

It was John. Sophie forced out yet another sigh. Seldom do things go as one would script them, and right now she didn't feel in the frame of mind to deal with John. But he was so cordial she could really see no recourse but to go with the moment. He materialized before her.

----I'll go straight to the matta', Sophie. I'm very sorry I didn't tell you about Job. It's just that I've seen so many die in the hospital and on the battlefield and most of them good friends, too. I have to tell ya', the pain is almost unbearable at times. It got to be that I'd rather be the one dead than to live with the losses. Bein' back home, I've seen a lot of sufferin' but not the kind that steals all hope like an early death. Then when I saw Job thea' it all came back to me. And as much as I didn't want to deal with it, I couldn't stand to see you suffa'. I care too much foa' you to let that happen. At least that was what I was thinkin' in that brief moment. I didn't have time to think it through moa' ca'efully. So, anyway, I hope you can foa'give me.

Sophie could feel the distant fire reflecting on her own face and she could see the moon in John's. Stephen had given her much the same kind of speech about his love and concern and she had not believed him. It was all in the eyes. They are the windows to the soul, and the curtains can not be drawn. In the windows that were Stephens eyes there was something cold like a draughty room. Yet, something in John's moonlit blue eyes made her believe he was sincere. There was a warmth beyond the blue twinkle that drew her to him.

And now the act that had so angered her endeared her to him. Still, her womanly instincts told her not to relent so easily even though she wanted to embrace him in that moment. The unquenchable tug that she felt made her feel like an ocean tide, and the reflected moon that she could see in the soft blue windows pulled her to the shore. The power of it alarmed her. She could see he was waiting for a response.

----Seeing that yoa' misguided actions were wrought out of yoa' conce'n foa' me how could I possibly count it against you? Yes, I fo'give you, John. But thea' ah' still some details we must attend to. I need to know what you have done with Job. We have a cemetery for all the se'vants, and I am shua' Job would want to be buried with his wife in the family burial place. That will be possible won't it?

----Thank you, Sophie, yes. He is in a very restful spot. I conducted a nice se'vice foa' him, best I could anyway unda' the circumstances.

----Will you take me thea' tomorrow?

----Are you shua'?

----Yes, I'm shua'.

The sheriff of Turkeytown, Joshua Weed, was in attendance as an invited guest. He was squat and a little rotund. He sported a bushy mustache, that when he spoke, it moved, because it covered his mouth. He approached and apologetically broke into the discussion between John and Sophie.

----John, I'm sorry to intrude. I beg yoa' pa'don too, Miss Sophie, but I need to speak to John on some urgent business.

He looked squarely at John and there seemed to be an urgency in his expression. Sophie noted too that John did not seem surprised.

----It appea's the sheriff needs to speak to me in private, Sophie, so if you'll excuse me.

He started to go and then flung a look back at Sophie as if he had forgotten something.

---- I hoped you might be my partna' foa' a dance oa' two this evenin'.

Sophie smiled sweetly.

----It would be my plezha'.

Out away from the light of the fire and the glow of the moon, a stealthy observer hid in the cover of the brush. It was not by accident that he skulked in the shadows and lay dumb under the cover they provided. His vision was fixed on the couple before him. He dared not move for fear of discovery with no good explanation for his presence. He seemed particularly intent on the young lady that stood not far from him. At least close enough that he could hear her speak. Jack, the Croft overseer, had seen and heard enough for this night.

The food was delicious. The pig was roasted to perfection, a Poland-China. It was in his honor that this party was held. Food was still scarce being so soon after the war, but this pig was bought and it was found to be a chicken eater. The previous owner was rather unscrupulous and sold the pig knowing his cannibalistic tendencies without divulging them. The Sewells soon discovered the pig's unwholesome habit and had to butcher him prematurely, thus the reason for the barbecue. In addition to the guest of dishonor, there was corn, biscuits and greens enough to satisfy the hungriest appetite. The fiddles were blazing feverishly, classic tunes of the Confederacy. The men were engaged in singing, "Three cheers for the homespun dresses Southern ladies wear" Sophie was glad she had not overdressed. A song exulting women for wearing the very poor, uncomfortable garments of war time would be very hard to hear while dressed in finery.

Stephen had disappeared and John had not been seen since their talk earlier. She wondered where each was, but for two very different reasons. John had looked so regal standing there by the fire. The war hero come home with an arm lifeless in one sleeve---a banner to a higher call. He seemed so principled, so devoted to what was good and right. Even his avoidance of the truth about Job was somehow chivalric even though she disapproved of his choice not to tell her. She could hardly see Stephen in the same light. He cared very much for position and money. He seemed like one who might compromise his most guarded beliefs if it might gain him advantage. It all seemed much clearer to her now. Or maybe he just seemed to pale further when placed beside John in comparison. Sophie had been sitting on the Sewell's front piazza with a few ladies who had been sharing stories of Yankee atrocities from friends and relatives all over the South. She had drifted off in a moment of ennui until George broke her reverie. John's gangly young brother addressed her abruptly.

----Heya Sophie. What eva' ah' you doin' hea'?

George was still in need of some refinement, sweet as he was. His schooling had been taken over by the War for Southern Independence. His instructors were too often brawlers and gamblers. His innocence was irresistible to the lower types who loved to get him in some sort of trouble.

----Why I was invited by yoa' sista' Susan, Georgie.

----Yoa' lookin' might beautiful tonight, Sophie.

He paused as he looked her first up and then down in a rather obvious gesture. He meant nothing by it, and in fact he probably had no idea he was in fact gawking. He quit staring and got back to talking.

---- I reckon ya' don't rememba' the promise ya made to me befoa' I left to fight now do ya?

----And what promise was that, Georgie?

----The one whea' you said you'd be my girl when I came home.

----Now Georgie, I do recall you askin', but I also remember sayin' I would pray foa' yoa' safe return. Thea' is a difference Georgie, although I am flatt'ed you asked.

Georgie grinned broadly as one who had tried to off with a stolen prize and had been caught.

----Aw shucks, Sophie. You do rememba'. Do you rememba' the ribbon you pulled from yoa' hai' and gave to me foa' luck?

----I do

Sophie paused for a moment looking about the Sewell's grounds.

----Georgie, have you seen yoa' brotha'?

----Who, Charles Henry? Why that boy's hustlin' up money shinin' and fixin' shoes. I swea' he's gonna be a me'chant or somethin' some day.

----No, Georgie, I meant John.

----Oh. He's back of the barn talkin' to a whole group of fella's. About what I don't know.

----Thanks Georgie, excuse me will you?

----Shua' Sophie.

Her female curiosity was getting the best of her and she did nothing to discourage it. She rose, picked up her dress and moved with rapid steps to the barn. She hesitated as she got to the back corner and heard low male voices.

----So all is set for tomorrow then?

----Yes, and of co'us secrecy is vital.

----Unda'stood.

There was a pause as the men stopped to listen like frightened deer.

----Who's thea'?

Sophie stepped out from around the corner as if she had only just arrived. In the illumination of the moon she could recognize several of the half-dozen men. There was Jack, their overseer, the sheriff, Joshua Weed, and John. All were now standing silent. John was the first to speak.

----Sophie

He seemed as if he didn't know what to say. In the brief moment of his hesitation the music began again loud and clear. John continued.

----It's the Virginia Reel. Could I trouble you foa' the last dance of the evening, Sophie?

He took her by the arm and escorted her to the pavilion where the laughter and merriment were reaching a crescendo. The lines were forming and partners were standing across from each other. John positioned himself in front of Sophie about three paces distant. Looking across the way she could not help noticing how distinct he looked between a pair of men on either side. He was taller, more winsome than anyone in attendance. He grew more handsome each time she saw him, and it was apparent she was not the only one to notice. As the head and foot couples were called to bow she observed that John seemed a little uncomfortable. She was quick to notice his arm that was held close to his coat. The swinging required would not be possible and he no doubt was concerned with how to proceed. His eyes met hers and it was clear each knew what the other was thinking. Sophie smiled knowingly as if to say, "Don't worry. I'll take care of it." John seemed relieved. The next call came and John stepped forward to swing with Sophie. He could not extend his withered arm so Sophie reached hers around his waist and pulled him close. She looked directly into his clear blue windows as they moved gracefully around to opposite positions. When it came time to cache' between the line of onlookers, they stepped forward and Sophie this time took John's atrophied hand in hers, and with light steps finished the reel under an archway of friendly arms. All was an air of gaiety, and Sophie with John at her side moved away from the music and back close to the fire. She had almost forgotten the gift she had intended to give and abruptly turned to face John as she remembered it.

----Oh, I had almost foa'gotten.

Sophie reached into her handbag and proffered the gift.

----Had you not come when you did yesterday on the road I shu'ely would have been ha'med. So while I was out I picked up this small token of my appreciation. I know it's not much since I do feel I owe you my life.

John accepted the gift, feeling a little embarrassed.

----I didn't help you foa' the hope of a rewa'd, Sophie. I do, howeva', appreciate the gift. You know you should have waited. You may someday be requi'ed to give a life foa' a life. You did say you feel that you owe me yoa' life?

Where was he going with this? To her questioning look he said:

----Who knows, I could be the one pinned down by some angry Yankees and you might have to chase them off.

She had thought for a moment he was intimating their possible future together. He was intent on her but there were no clues hidden in his stoic face. She decided to probe his thoughts.

----You know I would willingly give my life foa' you, John.

She paused to view his expression which was partially hidden in the darkness, and then strategically added.

----The Scripture is clea' that we are to no man be a debtor. And as I have said, I do owe you.

She was quite enjoying this play with words if indeed that was what was happening. She knew he had interest in her but how much she did not know. She waited for his move in this chess game of semantics. He moved swiftly.

----Ah, but you could ha'dly pay a debt with a life that is not enti'ely yoa' own. You have sworn it to anotha'.

Check....She was at a rare loss for words. Sophie had almost forgotten that Stephen had introduced himself as her fiancee'. How could she possibly explain it all right here, right now. She evidently had paused too long in response and John spoke out of turn.

----I can see from yoa' silence that it is true. Come Sophie, let me walk you to yoa' carriage.

He said it, smiling, but disappointment seemed to be in the tone of his voice. As they walked, she felt the need to say something. She couldn't just leave it there. She tried a brief explanation.

----I don't think you unda'stand, John. It is very complicated.

----You don't owe me an explanation, Sophie. I have some business to attend to early tomorrow. May I come in the afta'noon to escort you to the gravesite?

----Yes, thank you.

John helped her aboard and Tobias set out for Croft Plantation. Sophie mused on the evening thinking that it was the most fun she had had in a very long time, and that she enjoyed John's company very much in the little time she had been able to spend with him. Even Stephen's unexpected appearance could not dampen the night. She did wonder what became of Stephen after she had left him. She had not seen him after that time. Sophie had not had time to think about the conversation she had overheard earlier, but she could not imagine what such an assembly had in mind. Secret plans? Tomorrow? John, Jack and the sheriff among them. It was all very curious.

Into this evening filled only with the familiar sounds of the night came the unwanted sounds of another rider on an otherwise deserted road. Sophie turned behind her not knowing whether the one who approached, if he be only one, was friend or foe. From the apparent rapid pace she would know very soon. Before she could plan a course of action he was upon her. Jack reined alongside, he too coming home from the Sewell's, and offered to escort them the rest of the way home. Sophie was uncertain if she should be relieved.

Chapter Eight

There was a pall that shrouded the deep cuts of Owl's Hollow the following morning. At the base of a precipitous hill in the midst of a grove of willow oaks dripping with Spanish moss that added to the eeriness of the scene, five bleary-eyed, full- bearded men hunched around a light fire to fend off the morning cold. The rising smoke mixed with the low hanging fog to give the huddled men a ghost-like appearance. They could have been brothers, being so similar- medium build, rather stout, bearded, dirty and lewd. Even their bearings were the same in movement and in action. They were waiting for a visitor who would set them forth on yet another hellish deed that they were all too willing to carry out---for the right price. Each wore a coat of blue and had sworn allegiance to the Union which had emerged the victor. Each had a Springfield rifle resting in his lap in reddiness for a raid. All sought revenge on Southerners who carried on this war. Two were Alabamans who much to the shame of their brethren did not answer the call to defend their homes, but instead sided with the invaders. Two others were rebel deserters who hid in the hills during war to escape military judgment. The last was a Yankee, who seeing the lawless state of the South found an opportunity to don his uniform and plunder at will with little opposition. These five had raped, murdered, and thieved citizens of the South both free and slave since the end of the conflict. Sometimes their motivation was revenge, other times it was for loot. The backer for their latest actions had offered to pay them well, and they were anxious for his arrival and the settlement of the debt. Just last week they had drug a former Confederate soldier from his home, and in front of his parents shot him dead. They had proclaimed "justice served". As a light drizzle padded on downturned leaves, horses hooves thundered through the muddy lane that led to Owl's Hollow, the sole entry and exit to that den of thieves. It was not one rider but six, with hats set low, and brims dripping rain that rushed upon the startled band. Their mouths breathed smoke and their eyes were aflame with the heat of a coming battle. For most of them, this was not new. They were warriors late of possibly the greatest fighting force the world has known. They were Confederate veterans and their blood was up. Upon recognition of the raid, the rogues fled the only direction they could--straight up the hillside. They were on foot and they spread out as they climbed. They panted heavily and they ran with the fear of a hunted animal. The pursuers had dismounted and followed not far behind. It was good to see the Yankees running once again. Jack Arp stopped to fire and discharged his weapon. Missed. Sheriff Weed likewise took aim and fired. His aim was true. The fleeing fugitive fell in a heap with only a short, hoarse cry---then silence and no movement. One down. The others did likewise and two more of the scoundrels lay silent. Some shots were returned and the men halted in the cover of large trees. Sheriff Weed called out each man by name to give account.

----Jack?

----Yep

----Obadiah?

----Hea'

----Carl?

----Yea

----Jesse?

----Yep

----John?

No answer.

----John C. ? Damn. Anyone see John Huff?

A reply came from the overseer Jack.

----He was hangin' back when we came upon the camp. I lost sight of him.

The two bluecoats again took to flight up the ridge. The posse pressed on behind stopping briefly to check on the fallen three. They were all dead. It would save them the trouble of hangin' later. The two merged together and continued their flight as a pair. They had gained a considerable amount of distance on the pursuers and were nearing the top of the ridge. As they were plotting their course they were startled by an unexpected presence. John was perched behind an oak tree with the barrel of his gun resting on a branch. He addressed the glaring pair in a mocking voice.

----Well, if it isn't two of the Union's finest.

He could see they were reconnoitering the situation. Two of them, guns ready to fire, against a lone man with only one good arm. It was a chance they both knew they would take rather than swing from a tree. The one looking slightly older did the speaking, while his partner took two steps to his left to separate them.

----Those are some saucy words comin' from a one-armed man. How you figurin' on stoppin' both of us?

----You've heard say that one reb soldier's betta' than three Yanks haven't ya'? Well I'm willin' to prove it if you don't put down yoa' guns right now.

----Looks to me like you're only half a reb.

The robust, bearded man grinned a sharp-toothed grin as the echoes of the approaching posse resounded through the hollow. Recognizing time was short, the duo made their move. John's gun being trained on the older, the younger one raised his weapon. Before he could discharge, John wheeled the rifle on the branch and without chance to aim, fired rapidly. The single ball plucked at the center of the man's chest dropping him heavily to the earth. His single shot rifle being expended, John reached into his belt and drew his revolver as he tumbled to the ground. Even from the distance he could see the eyes widen on the face of the man turned target. The barrel that had been trained on John swiveled toward him as he fell. As he looked up and pointed the gun, he saw the black opening swing toward him and stop. John hastily squeezed the trigger, getting off the first shot. The second of the men yelped as the ball found its mark. The rifle that the target was holding soared through the air as if he had thrown it, discharging the slug as it left his hands. He was lying on the ground gripping his leg above a wound. John was hoping for the heart but had struck the thigh instead. The man was howling and writhing on the ground in obvious agony. In no big hurry the hunter sauntered over to where the hunted lay. The fracture was compound; the white bone protruding through the torn, swollen skin. It was a ghastly sight. Away from the battlefield, the wound seemed strangely out of place, sort of like a waltz being played during a hand to hand fight to the death. It was quiet except for the voices of the oncoming posse and the light patter of drizzle on open leaves. John stood over the bleeding Yank.

----Ain't ya' gonna' stop the bleedin'? You can't just let me die here.

The blood was gushing and he would surely die in moments if a tourniquet was not soon applied.

----I'll help you if you tell me what I need to know.

----Anything! Just help me for God's sake!

The life was spilling rapidly so John leaned close and asked,

----Who sent you to the Crofts to harass the young lady Sophie?

John, too, believed there was someone behind the attack. The voices of his comrades came welcome to his ears. He could hear Jack approaching more quickly than the rest. The overseer probably heard the shots and realized the pair had fallen upon one of his party and was rushing to his aid. The floundering man began to groan but answered wearily.

-----I don't recall. Some...ahhg...bigshot dandy.

Jack had found him and was rushing across an opening in his direction. He called out to John.

----John, wait, he's the only one left.

The eyes rolled back in the head of the wounded fugitive as he labored to form the words.

----...Pratt---Stephen Pratt is his name. Now help me, quick.

Pratt! He could hardly believe what he heard. He directed another question to the dying man.

----Why?

Nothing left. Jack arrived just in time to see John standing pensively over the last of the rogues. He was trying to piece it all together.

----Whew! Looks like we all made it out ok. It looked like you were gonna' finish 'em off. Wouldn't blame ya' of cou'se. I was tryin' to tell ya' he was the only one left to question, though. Did he say anything?

John thought for a brief moment and looked squarely at Jack wondering if he could be trusted. He did not know him well and he easily could be party to this, whatever *this* was.

----Nah, he didn't have a chance.

Jack replied,

----Too bad.

John looked up to see Jack's eyes fixed upon him. He reiterated the regret.

----Yeah, too bad.

The remainder of the posse arrived breathless at the top of the ridge. Sheriff Weed looked upon the fallen foe and checked any sign of life. He verbalized the obvious.

----Yep, he's dead.

He turned to John.

---- Shua' glad to see you alive, John. We thought you were done foa'. What happened?

----Well I guess It's just trainin', but when I saw high ground I just had to head for it. I knew they would flee up the ridge, so I just set up hea' and waited fo' 'em. I was goin' to haul 'em in but they challenged me. I told them one good reb was betta' than three Yanks.

.   John smiled and patted the bad arm, then added.

----Prob'ly three hundred thousand dead Yankees tellin' 'em that right now.

John did not care for killin' but he recognized warfare as the way of things even as a staple of scripture. Issues have been decided by combat since the dawn of time, and he did not figure that would change any time soon. The sheriff was anxious for answers. There were a lot of mysteries surrounding these men. Where was the loot they stole? Who else was involved in their actions, if anybody? He asked John,

----Did either of them say anything befoa' they died?

John was not one to lie. It was a source of pride to most Southerners he knew, rich or not that a man's word was his bond, and truth was ordered by God. He had never lied to his parents or the hired servants. It was not always easy to tell the truth, and his honesty had often landed him in trouble. But the negroes knew to trust his word because of it. And when he and his father had told them they were free to go, but that the lands and riches they invisioned would not be so easy to come by and the promises made by the government would likely not come to pass, they believed them. And they had been right. The poor servants had dreams of living like their masters and all of it given to them by the victorious Yankees who would take Southern property and turn it over to former slaves. "Forty acres and a mule", was the government's guarantee to the former slaves. The promise prompted many of them to leave the security of their plantation homes where they were at least cared for in search of riches that never came to fruition. Great hardships were endured by the Africans at the expense of freedom. For many it was an even more bitter pill. Nevertheless, John in the interest of justice and self preservation consented with himself to deceive. He answered the respected la wman.

----I guess we ah' left with a bunch of questions, sheriff.

There. Hopefully it would be left alone and John could find for himself what Master Pratt was up to.

Chapter Nine

Stephen heard the shots reverberate through the placid hollow. He knew what was afoot and he cursed himself for leaving such weighty matters to such a group of half-wits. He had done an about face and retreated to the preordained sanctuary of a wooded spur out Broken Arrow Road. In the event of trouble the clandestine meeting was to hastily move to this remote spot. In the two hours he had waited anxiously for some word, he had a lot of time to think things over. The rain had subsided but the sun had not yet pierced the dense foliage under which Stephen sat perched on a large flattened rock. His form was picturesque, yet the inner man was a mere distortion of the shell. All that is good and noble in men he could only muster but little. His motivations were those of the ambitious, and it was ambition that rived his soul. Still, it was not entirely his fault.   In   gaining   his   fortune   his   father   had compromised, cheated, extorted, along the way. He scoffed at the traditional Southerner's code and used it to his advantage. And his son had been there to watch-- and learn. It could not be said that the senior Pratt cared only for himself. Not since the birth of his only son. In his own skewed way he loved him and raised him in his own manner, much to the child's detriment. He had kept his son from the war by paying a doctor to declare him unfit, probably saving his life. He had given him everything to make his life comfortable even during the worst of times. And he arranged for him a good wife that complimented his lifestyle and education as well as add lucrative assets to protect his future. In spite of his seeming devotion however, Stephen's father was rash and demanding. He commanded compliance and showed the potential, even on a whim, to turn quickly on the children he fathered. They were afraid of him. Everywhere in Stephen's life was the imprint of his father's hand, and he daily bore the weight of it.

As he sat on the cool stone slab, he thought on the fullness of his life and what complications the present developments might hold. He knew the misfits would not be taken alive and their secrets, which were also his, would die with them. If by chance they were to be captured, their only hope would be a wealthy friend with some influence. No, they would not talk. Leaving one's future in the hands of such as these, though, held no comfort. The mere mention of his name would associate him with all the other misdeeds of the band which were no doubt numerous, and which he was not privy to. He had heard about the bushwackers through a friend who was a staunch Unionist from north Alabama. Although Stephen was not fully Union he was neither Confederate. He was of the most disliked of both sides-- whichever suited him at the time. The war, as he saw it, was going to cut into his cash flow, and he was most desirous that it not come.

Stephen's patience brought him dividends, but the drum of horses' hooves he had expected did not greet his ears. Instead, a dilapidated cart pulled by a pair of aged oxen came into immediate view. Stephen recognized the driver. It was Mildred, a wretched wisp of a woman graying into her waning years. She was a poor white woman of the lowest class. She had been widowed and then retreated to a mountain cabin where she cared for the bushwhackers as adopted sons. As she neared, Stephen could see she was heaving with heavy sobs. This was bad for sure. He tried to suppress his panic as he spoke.

----What happened?

----Theyz dead. Theyz all dead.

The old woman's eyes were watery slits and she shook her head as she spoke. She was hysterical.

----Calm down you wretch and tell me what happened.

She did not take offense. She knew what she was. She quieted and looked straight past Stephen as if the events were being played out in the air before her fixed eyes.

----We were about out of wood so I went foragin'. I heard the shots so I hid out off the road. I saw six men pass and when they were gone I went to see 'bout my boys. Ohhh...and when I got thea' theyz all was passed on away. What am I gonna' do now? What am I gonna' do now? All my boys is gone.

She was an eccentric old woman and her manner was odd. With ragged, cloudy eyes she looked to Stephen. It was obvious even to her that he was unconcerned for her grief, but rather he was consumed at the moment with his own problems. The hired thugs would be hard to replace, but that was not his greatest fear. He wondered if any of them had implicated him in any way. Stephen turned again to address the old woman.

----All of them were dead; are you sure?

She nodded deliberately. He directed another question.

----Who was in the posse?

----The only one I knowed fer sure was Sheriff Weed. The rest was all covered up.

That made sense. It was the local "Circle Gang" . Nathan Forests' doing. He organized groups of Southerners to protect the loyal citizens from the kinds of attacks carried out by the bushwhackers. He didn't know much about them, but he knew they were to meet in December to formally name the organization. He even knew that the meeting was to be held in either Pulaski, Tennessee, or Huntsville. And he also knew their justice was often swift and violent. He did not know who the members were, since they were a secret society, but he did know the sheriff was among their numbers. It would help to know who the enemy might be.

Leaving the gnarled woman to her own despair, Stephen mounted the marvelous horse and set out on the road to the Croft's. There he might find the answers he sought. He would rather face Sophie than the posse if the truth was out. She, he could manipulate and possibly persuade, that he in fact was not to blame. The posse, though, was a different matter. If any of the villains talked before they died, he would be hanged first and questioned later.

The brilliant steed gobbled up the short distance to the Crofts passing through steep ridges and open farmland along the way. He turned onto Croft Ferry Road and then down the narrow lane to the front of the expansive white home. His heart was pounding with the fear that he had been found out, the unexpected being more frightful than the confrontation that may wait. He would soon know. Sophie stood on the front piazza with her father. They saw him approach but there was nothing in their countenances that revealed foreknowledge. As he drew in upon them, to Stephen's great relief, a smile cornered on the face of the eldest Croft. He knew better than to look to Sophie for reassurance. She was curt as she greeted him.

----So nice to see you, Stephen.

Now at ease, he was amused by Sophie's mock enthusiasm in the presence of her father.

----And as always a shear delight to see you, Sophie.

Stephen bowed courteously. He turned to the pallid David Croft.

----And a good day to you, Sir.

Mr. Croft extended his quaking hand, and spoke in a rasping voice.

----Stephen, my good man. How is yoa' fatha'?

----Father is well and he sends his regards. He wished me to relay that the two of you have some business to tend to following some of the finest cuisine the South has to offer.

The Croft patriarch seemed pleased, and with a wink at Stephen he replied,

----I believe you also have some business *hea'*.

He laughed a bawdy laugh which sent him into convulsive coughing. Sophie stepped toward him but he raised his hand to ward her off.

----No, no, I'm fine, dea'. It's just a cough.

They all knew it was not so, but no one said a word. When he was again able to talk, Mr. Croft funneled his words to Stephen.

----Come with me to the fields. I have something to show you.

They excused themselves and ventured out together to the silent acres. The cotton had been harvested and the land was bare. The air was dense and the emerging sun was hot. David Croft stopped and sighed heavily.

----It has been a ha'd year, Stephen. The yield foa' this yea' is just ova' a hundred bales. I am heavily indebted to Ayers&Sons and I have a contract with the servants foa' part of the crop. I am finished. What I am trying to say, Stephen, is that all of this is yoa's if you want it. I don't want to trouble Sophie with all this, but I've come down with consumption. I don't have long and I need to know she'll be taken care of. I need to know yoa' intentions. You know I would have you as my own son and you know too that it would please yoa' fatha' and me both if the two of you should marry. But I don't know how you feel about it. And thea' is one otha' matta'. It has come to my attention that Sophie is becoming very friendly with oua' neighba' John Huff. I'm concerned that if you don't move quickly, her affections may turn to him. Don't get me wrong; he is nice enough, but he has nothing to offa' my Sophie. Do you see what I'm sayin', Stephen?

Stephen's mind was turning like a wagon's wheel with all that was set before him. He was being pressed to move with Sophie. He was offered the plantation. John Huff whom he had met on the road with Sophie was apparently interested in her. His eyes were cold set as he spoke. They did not betray the lie he uttered.

----Yes, sir. I do. It is my full intention to ask Sophie to be mine, with your permission of course.

----Ah, wonda'ful. You most ce'tainly have my blessing.

----Begging your pardon, sir, but are you certain Miss Sophie will welcome my proposal?

----She has given me no hint that she objects to the union. Besides, she would be a foolish girl to decline yoa' offa'. She has too great a recognition of her responsibilities to her sista's and her home to wait on some foolish book notion of love. She will marry you and will be a very good wife and motha'; you will see.

----She is your daughter. I would expect no less.

They were standing as two solitary figures in the freshly picked fields. The ground looked littered with scraps of white paper from the small fibers left upon the viney branches. It was Saturday and the servants had just finished their half day work as they always had under the old system. There was some commotion on the lane that led to the house. It was time for a weekend favorite---the horse race. The pair made their way to the clouded road and waited for the start of the first event. Tobias, the driver, sat erect on an unblemished horse, with Cain, a field servant close beside him on a large white mare dotted in caramel. The two beamed and grinned white teeth through perspiring faces. Bets were made all around at the last moment. Stephen cast his lot with Tobias. One wiry field hand heard him place the bet and troubled him for his choice.

----Marse' Stephen, 'dat nigga's so stiff in 'dat saddle, 'Dat anim'l 'taint goin' no weya fo' sho'.

All present had a good laugh at Tobias' expense. On signal, the horses bolted in a frenzy of movement. Cain jumped to an early lead on his spotted white horse, but Tobias, looking very determined, closed the gap as the two neared the dark mass of gathered onlookers. At the races end, the horse ridden by Tobias edged out the one ridden by Cain, much to the dismay of the field hands present. Money changed hands among the disgruntled negroes; nevertheless, they all went away content with the good sport they had witnessed. Tobias was especially proud, and he maintained his erect posture throughout the day. The crowd dispersed, many of the servants going back to the quarters, many others taking weekend leave to other plantations as they always had. Passes were still necessary, for the military law was still in the practice of hauling off negroes who were without papers. There was also the threat from the lawless bands who associated themselves with the "Circle" which was formed to protect the rights of all Southerners. These vigilantes had become overzealous in their pursuit of the Africans. Stephen recalled that some of them had come robed and hooded to the Croft house one evening when he and his father were there, calling for Cain to be brought out and whipped. Master Croft protested vehemently that he could speak for Cain's character and assured them he had not done what they accused. The old man further said that they would have to fight through him before they take Cain. "We're not willing to trade a white man's life for a nigga'", they had reasoned. And off they rode. Mr. Croft talked to some official members of the gang the following day, and they had known nothing of the act. It was all very unfortunate. Had the Union law in force recognized the growing problem of idle and poor negroes acting violently against their former benefactors, then the KuKlux would have only to deal with the criminal Yankees they were organized to combat. Loyal Confederate veterans were being taken from their homes and killed by the victors with complete immunity. The Clan became the law in a lawless age. And it was this law that Stephen feared most. In addition to the murder of a beloved family servant, which he did not specifically order, he had ordered an attack on a young southern girl, which would be reason enough for the Clan to string him high from a sturdy tree.

The two men strode back to the "great house" discussing the horse race they had just witnessed. Sophie was nowhere in sight, so Stephen excused himself and bid farewell to Mr. Croft, vowing to return on the morrow to speak to his eldest daughter.

As he passed out onto the Croft Ferry Road, he began formulating a plan. The introduction of this John character could prove helpful. Stephen urged his horse, for he had another meeting he could not miss. He made his way quickly to the Coosa, where the *Laura Moore* lay in wait.

Among the passengers sitting in the posh upper deck reserved for the first class, was a voluptuous belle with thick blonde curls and dazzling green eyes that seemed to garnish her face much like the decorative garnish on the plate before her. She appeared anxious as she waited for the familiar form of someone she would recognize through a thick river fog from a distance. He had said he would meet her here after he attended to a small matter with some friends. He was overdue and she was concerned. She looked out windows and fidgeted with her hair.

Rising on the staircase opposite, there appeared a shock of dark hair and then a perfectly symmetrical face that looked to have been carved from a flawless piece of marble. He was impeccably dressed and was no stranger to the first class accommodations. Stephen, with quick, graceful steps slid into the chair set for him and spoke in a feathery voice to the waiting beauty.

----Forgive me, Anna, for my tardiness. Things have gotten a bit messy.

----I was so worried. I abhor that you must deal with those vipers. I imagined all sorts of terrible things happening to you. Did you have to go to the Crofts again? You know how I dislike you spending time with the woman you are supposed to marry. This is getting so terribly difficult. I don't know how much more of this I can stand, Stephen.

Her eyes were like a dam holding back a deluge of tears, and Stephen was anxious to broach his business and hopefully to put her at ease.

----Anna, the attempt to force a sale of the plantation is not going to come to pass. The old man seems determined to keep it, and now, without the the means to intimidate them, I fear we must pursue another course. I had hoped that the Crofts would sell to my contact and move far away from here. We would have been free to marry and live out our lives as we wished. With the railroad coming through one side of the property and the river on the other, distribution of our gins and our own cotton would have made us wealthy beyond our fondest dreams. Now with Sophie's father so determined to hold on to the property, and this John Huff around to give support, they will never sell.

Just then, a simple waiter dressed in white, rounded the table quite unexpectedly to refill the water glasses. He seemed out of place, a white man doing the work of servants, but the war had toppled the regular order of things and now anything unusual seemed to be common. His movements were stiff and mechanical. He began to pour the water when Stephen reeled on him.

----Can you not see that we wish to be undisturbed! How would you like to be picking fields for your living?

The man shrank back and removed himself to a place nearby where he could be called upon if necessary. Stephen leaned his head over the table between two brass candlesticks and continued his conversation with Anna.

----I suppose I will tell Mr. Croft that I will not marry his daughter, nor will I save his land. Then I will tell my father I intend to defy his wishes and marry the woman of my choice. He will wish me well and send me away to start on my own.

----Stephen, you know the money doesn't matter to me.

He leaned closer.

----But it does to me, Anna. You have never been without it, my love. If you were waiting on tables like this poor sot, you would feel differently.

Anna looked puzzled by his remarks. The words made her feel very uneasy.

----What are you telling me, Stephen?

Stephen was making reference to the same waiter who was conversing with two other white-clad workers. Neither was aware that he did not listen to the small circle he was attached to, but rather he hung on the words of the couple speaking intimately behind him. The slight waiter heard the name of someone that meant something to him, and listened with keen interest to the conversation which involved him.

----Don't be alarmed dear. I only wish to convey to you that I have no intention of living in squalor with you. We will have *everything* we have strived for.

Anna was not comforted by his explanation. She was not so sure that if forced to choose that he would not make wealth his bride. And with good reason. Stephen himself had a fleeting thought. Sophie did not appeal to him, but he could learn to live with her. She was, without question, very attractive.

----Stephen, what of the men you hired? You said we could no longer count on them.

----All dead.

----So what does that mean?

----It means that we will not be retaining their services any longer. It also means that our involvement with them is no more a worry.

---What do we do now?

----Mr. Croft has offered me the plantation if I marry Sophie. He is very sick and will die soon. He is trying to secure the property.

----So what does that mean for us, Stephen?

----It means that we will soon have all that we want, Anna. I wish it were easier, but you know how my father is. Unless I play this game with him, he will write me off completely. We would be left with nothing. He must believe I have every intention of marrying Sophie. It is she who will refuse. Unfortunately, while her father is alive she is, like me, unlikely to defy her father's wishes. Although her reasons are a touch more noble, they are no less binding.

----I just wish it were over Stephen. I don't like pretending this way.

----Very soon, Anna. Very soon.

Stephen leaned across the table and kissed her forehead gently. He bade her farewell and exited the elegant state room of the large steamship. Anna watched him go. She was uneasy with the words he had spoken. Anna had hoped that she and Stephen would soon marry. The latest developments would delay things. The Croft plantation meant little to her, but Stephen was set on it, so she went along with his scheming. By now it was beginning to unsettle her. The waiter, seeing her, moved jerkily to her table.

----Anything moa' foa' you, ma'am?

----No thank you.

----Very well

He reached to take her undisturbed plate and the sleeve of his left hand withdrew to reveal a shocking sight. His gauzed arm was oozing through the wrap, and the injury, if it be that, seemed to extend quite some distance beyond what could be seen. From his movements it was evident the soars had racked his entire body. It looked as though he had been severely burned. She felt compassion for him, not only for the pain he must have been enduring, but for the way Stephen had spoken to him.

Stephen, meanwhile, was considering his options as he parted. His love for Anna was something that he could learn to live without. Losing her would hurt, without question, but living a life of penury was far less seemly. He decided to be patient. If he could have it all his way, he would surely prefer it. Maybe her father would deteriorate quickly. Maybe Sophie would then be willing to sell and move into town. Stephen did not like leaving things to chance.

Chapter Ten

----If only all of life were a dance.

Sophie sighed as she spoke the words to the cool morning. It was a perfect time of day to be out. The lines of the August dawn were sharp and in full focus. All that touched her skin was soft cotton and a light breeze that was tepid as bath water. The view from the front piazza was serene. The dusty ribbon of road beyond was mute. And the chatter of some Carolina wrens was like a hedge, muffling the voices of the distant negroes. She turned her head to the West and could see. A blot covered the horizon. An omen, she believed. Every dance must end like every glorious morning. You are left wishing for another, and try to weather the storms in between. Until you can dance again. She wondered if John might find such thoughts silly. She doubted it. For a man of action he also seemed to be one of thought. Just now he may be up to attend to whatever secretive business he was discussing with of all people, Jack. Before she could speculate further, she was greeted by her maidservant, Sadie.

----Mornin' Ma'am. I was ast' to knows what ya' be havin' foa' breakfast.

----I'll not be having breakfast this morning, thank you, Sadie.

Sophie started to ask if her chamber pot had been tended to this morning. She had almost forgotten that Sadie had decided that it would no longer be her responsibility now that she was free. Many of her former slaves had created their own work days, not quite understanding what it was to work under contract.

Sophie was left with little choice but to endure the slow transition to wage labor. If only all the servants had the opportunity Job had. She remembered that John had agreed to take her to his burial sight this day. She was not sure when he might come. She did know it would have to be after his business this morning. She could not even guess what it might be, but she desperately wanted to know what would bring together such an unlikely trio of men. She did not have the trust for Jack that her father held. Any man who showed no interest in marrying and lived among negroes as he did should be taken with caution. He boasted endlessly that he would some day be a planter himself, and even the depressed state of things could not deter his optimism.

Sophie had a wild thought. The sun was now blotted out from the rapidly approaching storm. The smell of rain was all about as she rose abruptly and hurried down the stairs. She made her way to the back of the house and peered out the window. As luck would have it, she could see that Jack was mounting his horse to leave. Seeing him dash away, she rushed out, still in her nightcbthes, and hair streaming unbridled behind her. She startled Silas, the stable hand, as she bolted into a stall.

----Miz' Sophie, whats in the Lord's good name you doin' ? If yuz' was a nigga' yo daddy had of sold you by now. You can't take that ho'se.

----That's why you won't tell him, Silas.

----I'z always cleanin' up yo messes, Miz Sophie. I don't want no wippin' or no sellin'.

Silas stood like a gate in front of the excited horse.

----I would never let that happen, Silas. Besides, yoa' free now, rememba'? Now help me up.

He shook his large round head and moved to help Sophie aboard. His face had the look of an exhausted parent who had lost yet another battle with a willful child.

----I must hurry, Silas, or I won't catch up.

----Who'z you catchin', Sophie? And wher'z you goin'?

Sophie was upon the massive animal and Silas stood looking helpless at her side. Before she could bolt, she became aware of someone coming 'round the stable wicket. It was her father. Silas shrank back to the corner, guilty and awaiting judgment. The eldest Croft looked first to Silas and then addressed his own spirited daughter.

----Sophie, what ah' you doing?

----Just going foa' a ride, Papa.

----So why the big rush then? You ah' still in yoa' night clothes.

----I was trying to beat the rain.

Her father grinned broadly which illicited no response and an obstinate look from Sophie who was determined to stick to her story. He looked again to Silas.

----Is that correct, Silas?

Without looking up, Silas could feel the hard stare of father and daughter.

----She tol' me she'z goin' fo' a ride sih'.

David Croft raised an eyebrow and spoke again to his very relieved oldest child.

----I do not know how you garner such loyalty from the servants who do not fea' you. I must say I do doubt yoa' explanation, howeva'.

He looked again at Silas who had not yet raised his head. Sophie gave no response. Mister Croft seemed to be amused with his daughter's attempts to conceal her actions.

----Come with me, Sophie. Thea' is a matta' of importance we must discuss.

He again broke into spastic coughs as he turned. He spoke peremptorily, allowing no room for refusal. As desperately as she wished to follow Jack, she could not refuse Papa. Silas, with a scolding look, helped her down and she followed her beloved father out into a drizzling rain. Before she left the faithful servant she mouthed the words, "thank you". She then caught up to her slow moving parent and took his arm.

----Let's hurry to the house, Papa. You'll catch yoa' death of cold.

He did not alter his pace.

They entered through the back and were received by Sadie who wrapped them both in a blanket. They made their way to the velvet sofa and sat. Sophie waited for her father to broach his business. His weathered face showed his anguish as he raised his head to speak.

----I cherish you Sophie and yoa' sisters as God's greatest gift. He has seen fit to bless me fa' beyond what I could eva' deserve. That is why it pains me so to have to tell you...

Sophie's eyes widened at the recognition of bad news. How bad she was afraid to know. She held her breath and could hear the rattling of her Papa's chest in the momentary silence.

----I'll be leaving you soon , Sophie.

She knew he was not speaking of a trip. Tears welled in her eyes as she spoke the denial that was the hope in her heart.

----We'll sell hea' and go to the sea. The air thea' will heal you; I know it.

----It is too late foa' me my dea'. But we must talk of you and yoa' sistas'.

For the second time in as many days, Sophie began to cry. She wanted to be strong for Papa, but she just could not hold back the deluge of tears that flooded from her eyes. He began again slowly.

----I'm afraid thea' is moa' bad news. Even at a good price oua' crop this yea' will leave us heavily in debt to Ayers and Sons. They have demanded payment by the fi'st of next month or will foreclose on our prope'ty.

----Very well then. We can take you to Mobile to recova'.

----Listen Sophie, I would neva' su'vive the trip. I want foa' you and the girls to stay hea'. Thea' is a way.

----And how is that, Papa?

She sensed what was coming and she suppressed the volatile outburst that was welling up inside her.

----I spoke to Stephen, yeste'day. He fully intends to propose to you very soon. I told him you would accept his offa'.

----You should know better than to speak foa' me, Papa.

How could he know that this response was a guarded one given the emotions that were broiling in her even now. Sophie was struck hard at the news of her father's impending death, even though it had not come as a great surprise. One can never be ready for such finality. David Croft continued undaunted.

111

----His capital would prese've this plantation foa' you and yoa' sisters. Not to mention that he cares very much foa' you. Thea' is not an unmarried young woman in all Montgomery who would refuse his affection and his fatha' is my oldest friend. You don't have much in the way of choices, Sophie, if you wish to live the kind of life you have grown accustomed to.

He had summoned enough strength to make his point clearly and forcefully, shrugging off the mantle of fragility long enough to make himself heard.

----But I do have a choice, Papa. You must confuse me with oua' slaves.

He was by now familiar with her caustic retorts.

----Why have you offered no resistance, knowing Stephen's fatha' and I have spoken often of yoa' union?

It was a question she should have foreseen, but at present had no good answer for.

----I don't know, Papa. But I do know how I feel in this moment. I do not desia' to marry Masta' Pratt. I am sorry if I disappoint you.

His question still bounced about in her brain. She, in spite of her fierce independence, had dreaded the thought of her father's disapproval. Especially in light of his recent illness. Now when he was most ill, she openly defied his wishes. She had long believed she would indeed marry Stephen, even if she did not love him. She had never felt a reason to object. It was her father that supplied the answer she inevitably would have found herself.

----This is about John Huff isn't it?

Again Sophie was unprepared, still lost in a thoughtful state. She had no reply so he continued in a more tender vein.

----Dea' sweet Sophie. It is easy to love a war hero. But a broken hero can not put a roof ova' yoa' head. Much less care foa' yoa' sisters.

Sophie wondered how he had concluded she was in love before even she had. And how did he know about John? She searched quickly for a smart reply. It was a discussion that might decide her fate.

----Papa, did you love motha'?

He knew he had lost in securing his will with that one simple question.

----With all my heart, Sophie.

----And did you choose her to be yoa' wife?

----With some urging from yoa' grandfatha', yes. But yoa' grandparents were an arranged marriage you know. They grew to love each otha' very dearly. That was my hope foa' you and Stephen. Stephen is moa' suited to yoa' upbringing, Sophie. It is an impo'tant thing to consida'.

----Then you will leave it to me to consida' then, Papa?

He smiled reluctantly in affirmation. Having sensed victory, she went on.

----Very well then. Let's now concentrate on getting you betta'. Aunt Molly will see you to bed.

Sophie's mammy who had suckled her as an infant had stepped in to hear her words and now aided the feeble Master to his quarters. The stout woman with round face and colorful turban gently leaned him against herself and nearly carried him up the stairs.

----Don't you worry none Miss Sophie, massah' is in the care of Aunt Molly now. If I could keeps you safe, I could surely chase the devil away from Massah'.

The discordant looking pair disappeared at the top of the stairs allowing Sophie to express openly the full weight of her despair. She fell in a heap onto the sofa and buried her face in its velvety softness. A managerie of thoughts pressed in upon her, beginning with her dear mother. Her loss was a devastating blow and now she would have to watch her father die. She did not think she could bare it alone. And then there was her home. It would surely be lost. Where would they all go. All the radiant, shining faces of the servants looking to her for care. She did not want more responsibility. She wanted to be carefree, listen to the laughter of healthy children and live out her days with someone who would care for her. There was one bright spot. She had been up front with her feelings about Stephen, and at least she was not condemned to live with a man she did not love. And it was no small consolation. The hope of love and companionship lifted her spirits. She did not know that she loved John, but she certainly liked him very much. And as little as she knew about being in love, she knew it must be a start.

Three loud knocks echoed through the halls of the Croft plantation home. Quinton, in his customary formal way advanced to the entrance hall and opened the heavy oak door. Sophie wiped away her tears and turned just in time to see John walk into the entrance. He seemed a little ill at ease standing in the doorway. She heard him state his business to Quinton.

----I have come foa' Sophie. Is she hea'?

Both men turned to witness her approach. She could see Quinton was grinning, not bothering to disguise his pleasure at seeing someone other than Stephen call on his misses. Sophie stepped lively to the door. She had almost forgotten she was still in her night clothes from her failed attempt to follow Jack. She quickly altered her route to advance up the staircase.

----If you'll excuse me I'll be down in a moment.

John held his black felt hat in his hand and nodded without word. He looked a bit embarrassed, as if he had seen more of her than was proper. Sophie noted however that it did not keep him from spying her as she ascended the stair. Her hair was not yet pinned over her ears and so it bounced freely as she bounded up like a child at play. She entered her room and jarred the door enough to hear any overspoken words she might spear. The revered butler closed the door and stood beside John in the entrance. He spoke softly to the visitor.

----I knows why you hea'.

John looked startled as if a secret he thought he alone knew had returned to his ears.

----You do?

----I do. And I want to offa' my help.

----Oh. And what do you plan to do?

----Whateva' massah' needs.

----I'm not shua' what you mean.

John thought for a moment that his interest in Sophie must be terribly obvious, almost forgetting himself the reason he had come.

----Job was my friend massah' Huff. We spent many nights huntin' togetha' I knows the spot he wished to call his own.

----I see now. I would welcome yoa' help. It will be a thankless choa' I can assure you, though. Can you keep Sophie at a comfortable distance? I don't think she has any idea what she has requested to do. The sight would trouble her foa' a long time to come

----Sho' 'nough done. I'z a little sup'stitous my self. I'll keep her plenty fa' back.

----Easia' said than done. Sophie may try to grab a shovel and do the job he'self.

They both laughed at the real possibility of such a happening.

----I know Tobias an' Silas have offered to help and they iz mo' sup'stitous than me. But they still want to help. They wuz good friends, too.

Quinton had allowed his formal speech to lapse, something he never did with Stephen. John exuded an ease of manner which, after his initial entrance, caused those about him to relax-including the servants.

Sophie had finished dressing and this time stepped lightly down the staircase. Her dress was a simple one. It was avocado and slightly worn- enough to be her most comfortable day dress. It would be appropriate for the work ahead. The collar plunged just below the neckline and its edges extended out to the ends of her delicate shoulders. Her long locks were pulled behind her, just covering her ears. She could see John there still in the doorway holding the black felt. He was casually dressed but neat. His hair looked as if he had been caught in the rain. He was partially shaven so that he looked quite rugged, rather a muss, and he seemed a little fuller in the body than he did just yesterday. His blue eyes seemed to glow as he looked up to where she was. She lost no time in indulging her curiosity.

----I see you finished yoa' business this mo'ning quickly. You caught me quite unprepared. You will foa'give my appearance?

John addressed her as she reached the bottom.

----Yes, I hope I am not too early. The business was a small matta'. I hope it doesn't change yoa' plans foa' the day.

----Oh no. Some unpleasant things must be attended to whetha' we wish to see to them oa' not. Quinton, has Tobias a wagon ready?

----Yes, Miss Sophie.

----I'll be riding with Mr. Huff. You will follow with the otha's?

----Yes, ma'am.

John stepped aside and allowed Sophie to pass through the elaborate doorway and pause at the wagon. She turned to look at the long narrow pine box in the back. John helped her up into the wagon, seated himself, and they embarked. There was a moment of awkward silence as the wagon lurched out onto the familiar road past the lovely magnolia and the spot where Job had fallen. Sophie broke the stalemate.

----I had a wonde'ful time last night, John.

Since they had not spent a great deal of the evening together, John was not certain if she was crediting him for her enjoyment.

----So did I, Sophie. I must say dancing with you was the highlight of my evening.

He said it without looking at her, and waited for a response.

----The rest of yoa' night was that bad?

He chuckled, amused at her words.

----On the contrary, it was altogetha' an enjoyable time. And foa' you?

----It was not without interest. I enjoyed the company of yoa' sista's and Georgie of course. But the evening nea'ly turned soua' when Stephen showed up.

117

----Stephen, yoa' fiancee'?

Now John turned to look her full in the face. Now she could say what she wished to say last night. She had directed the conversation adroitly to this moment.

----About that, John. Stephen addressed himself as my fiancee' because oua' fatha's have been planning oua' marriage foa' some yea's. Thea' is a great deal moa' to it, but all that aside, I told my fatha' just this mo'ning I have no intention of marrying Stephen.

John's face remained expressionless, yet the brightening of his eyes was almost perceptible when she spoke the words. And then he asked,

----Does Stephen know this?

----He will very soon.

Each looked at the other for a prolonged silent moment. Sophie felt the beating of her heart must surely be audible as she gazed upon his countenance. A sudden jolt of the wagon directed both to the road ahead. The plantation home was now just out of sight and John pulled the cart to a halt.

----We're thea'.

Sophie looked about for sign of the grave. The wagon behind reined in and its three inhabitants fell hushed in either fear or reverence. John explained.

----He is thea' in the field of heal-all. I thought it might be a fitting place.

John gestured and Sophie could see the trampled flowers and soft dirt at pathway end. Quinton, Tobias and Silas were at first hesitant. There heads were low and shoulders slumped. With an act of resolution, Silas, the largest of the three, stepped down and out onto the trodden path. Tobias helped John lift the pine box and

118

the three with shovels and shroud stepped through the trampled purple flowers. Quinton held back with the sullen Sophie. All three stood silent over the disturbed earth. John issued directions.

----Any of you done this befoa'?

They shook their heads.

----Well, I have. If you have to vomit step aside and do so. No shame in it. Dig carefully. When we get to the body throw the shroud ova' top and then tuck it unda'neath. Silas and I will lock hands beneath his back and you can take his feet, Tobias. Then we'll put him in the box.

Once again John began to dig. The two quaking Africans muttered pious offerings of "sweet Jesus" and "protect us Lo'ad" as if they expected some spiritual manifestation right before their bulging eyes. They were soon upon the torso of Job and the wool blanket. The vaporous body gasses loomed up and the acrid stench sent both the servants into violent upheaval. John continued scraping the dirt from the strewn cover. The others returned very shaken to a partially exposed corpse already in the early stages of decay. Still silent, but faces wet with tears, the friends of the deceased quickly wrapped the remains and hoisted them into the crude box. Sophie observed from a distance, glad she had not insisted on helping. In a moment they were reembarked with Job in tow.

---- It would seem you put some thought into yoa' place of burial foa' Job.

----Every man should have some dignity in death. I said a few words I hope were appropriate. I didn't know he would so soon be resu'rected.

John paused and asked.

119

----What will happen now?

----We have a cemetery for all the help. Thea' will be a late evening burial. All the negroe funerals ah' conducted late at night by torch light. I will attend of cou'se and you would be most welcome. That is if you don't have urgent business again this evening.

They crept passed the bonum apple trees that had provided John with the pleasant memory days ago and again the sweet scent drifted to him. She was fishing for information and he knew it. He decided to leave her guessing.

----I will be thea'.

----Yes, I believe you will be. You seem to be showing up a lot just when I need you.

----And do you need me then tonight?

----Very much.

----Then Hell could not bar the way.

They had reached the Croft lands and the family orchard was in sight. Sophie pressed John to stop and sent the others on with the cart and Job.

----"We will walk the rest of the way home", she told them as they hurried off.

They walked side by side and Sophie stopped beneath a peach tree ripe with fruit. Her body shook with anticipation and the feeling of the moment. Something was happening and she was no longer directing it. It was goading her. She began to ramble about the history of the orchard. John grasped her gently by the arm and turned her to face him.

----Sophie, I don't think I thanked you prope'ly for yoa' kind gift. Even moa' I need to thank you foa' making coming home something to always look foa'ward to as long as you ah' around. Yoa' welcome was very warm as is yoa' heart.

He reached his hand to cup her face and she thought for a moment her legs would not sustain her. She brought her hand to his and lifted her eyes to meet him in an obvious invitation. And he understood. He leaned his handsome head and pulled her face close to his, pressing his lips gently to hers in a tender kiss. With her eyes closed her senses were heightened and she could smell the peachtrees all about intermixed with the musk of his body. She became lost in the wonder of the sensation and just before she gave herself permission to yield completely to his kiss, he withdrew. She remained motionless with her vision of the world around her obstructed by her closed lids and by the images of a surreal existence that was without pain and that felt only pleasure. His voice did nothing to vanish the dream, but instead made it seem far more real.

----I hope I was not out of orda', Sophie. I sometimes act without thinking as you ah' well awa'e.

----If anyone was out of orda', John it was I. Had I made it any moa' clea' that I wanted you to kiss me, someone could have questioned my purity.

----I won't tell you how long it's been since I kissed a woman 'cause I don't want you to feel sorry foa' me, but I can tell you that a kiss neva' felt more pure than the one I just had.

----For a man of war you shua' know how to flatta' a lady, John Huff.

----My warring days are ova', Sophie. I had my fight for honor and it was an empty one. I gained glory foa' myself, but the cause I dedicated myself to is lost. So, I figure now that I will choose my fights. I'm guessin' that if I eva' hope to kiss you again, I may find myself in anotha' fight. One that may be as deadly.

----Whateva' do you mean, John?

Before John could reply, Jack Arp came riding at a fevered pace through the orchard. With the soft red dirt flying about, he came to a halt very near the couple.

----Is something wrong, Jack?

----Sorry to intrude, ma'am, but it's yoa' fatha'

Sophie was visibly shaken. She asked the question she feared the answer to.

----Is he all right?

----He's alive. But he can't get up.

----Take me to him.

She turned to John as she was helped upon the horse.

----Foa'give me. Will I see you tonight?

----Yes, When do you need me hea'?

Jack was staring coldly at John. He interposed.

----Sophie, you might want to cancel yoa' plans this evenin'.

The horse was jittery sensing the excitement of those around him. He would not stay still, but shook his shimmering mane and pranced in circles. It was clear Sophie did not want to leave John with no time for their meeting, but the horse was being difficult and Jack was trying to make plans for her. She could not will her mind to focus. John settled it.

----I will come at midnight.

She could not help but notice that Jack seemed disturbed at John's presence, and it didn't seem to fit, especially since they had worked together on some secretive affair this morning. She hadn't the time to think on that just now. Her papa was in trouble. Sophie

122

was afraid for her father, and at the same time troubled for herself. The trials of life seemed to stalk her, and when the joys of this world were within her reach, some tragic event snatched them from her grasp. As she dashed off on the back of Jack's horse she thought on her musings of the morning. If only all of life were a dance.

Chapter Eleven

John had covered the short distance to the Croft plantation home in just a few minutes. He had wished to be by Sophie's side, but felt it was not yet appropriate as she was certainly with her father. He had taken the wagon which had been wrested of its cargo and returned home to wait out the remainder of the day until he could again be with the woman that so captivated him. He smiled as he thought about his bold move earlier. Spontaneity certainly had its rewards. He felt pretty proud of himself. There was the same sense of victory he had at Shiloh when the 22nd had performed well. He had won her affections and the word itself implied a conquest. And yet he knew he would not be satisfied with winning the battle. It was not the winning that would fill up the empty places in him. It was the having and holding.

As he sat at the end of the circuitous path that terminated at the family springhouse, he splashed the cool fresh spring water in his face and hair. It seemed not only to cleanse him outwardly, but to cleanse his mind as well. When the water drained from his face and dripped into the lipid pool beneath, his thoughts seemed to rise above the haze that often distorts them. He wanted Sophie as his wife. It was a clear and simple vision that he knew would transform his life in countless ways. And might end it. So be it then. There was a time not long ago, during the war, that dying was a preferred option. Living was such toil that he had become reckless in battle. His life, he believed, would be better ended than to always fear the minnie ball that might take it from him. And now the full, richness of living was within his grasp. In his despair he could not believe he would ever again experience the joy of life. Without Sophie, he believed it could be that way again. Had he the hope of her love while going into battle he would have feared more for his life. And now, Stephen Pratt has been made an enemy. He would certainly be in danger for interfering with whatever plans the man from town had for Sophie.

The nearby chickens cackled, that being their only utterance, and above, in the apex of the plateau, his brothers and sisters played joyfully 'round the walnut trees. Charles Henry had not yet started working in the fields, being too young, and he was engaged in tormenting his three younger siblings with war games. Since he had no younger brothers, and the older ones, Georgie and William were tending to the corn, Charles was forced to play with Mary, Melissa, and Georgia or play alone. John looked to the top of the six foot wall of earth that lay on the opposite side of the path and saw Charles there looking down at him. John motioned to him and Charles bounded along the crooked path.

----Charles, when ah' you gonna' stop pretendin' that yoa' sista's ah' Yankees and quit shootin' at 'em?

----But, John, you said that the Yankees was nothin' but a bunch 'a girls.

----Yea, well that was befoa' they shot me. Truth is the Yankees are a bunch of girls with guns. And that makes 'em doubly dangerous.

Charles looked at his sisters as if he were trying to picture them shooting at him. The image seemed not to be consistent with what he had hoped for his game.

John had opened his shirt to allow for the water. His darkened neck and chest were exposed, and his right shoulder was left partially visible revealing one of his two chest wounds.   Charles was staring hard at the circular area of disturbed flesh. It was dark as a walnut on the ground above, and very round. He was polite enough not to ask questions, but not aware enough to realize he was gawking awkwardly. John answered the unspoken question.

----I got that at Shiloh. Little close to the heart, isn't it?

Charles now looked to John, having fully assessed the wound.

----Did it hu't?

----Not as bad as the second one.

John patted the other side of his chest.

----The surgeon ruled out amputatin' which was a great relief. But then they dressed the wound. Thea' was no need to probe for the ball- it went clean through. They took a piece of silk, fed it through the hole, and pulled it out the otha' side to clean it. That part hu't a bit. I didn't fuss though, 'cause the guy next to me was gettin' his a'm cut off, and he was pretty quiet. He just kinda' groaned and prayed a lot.

Charles grimaced at the gruesome thought.

----Did ya' get the Yankee that shot ya'?

----Neva' had a chance, Charles, but I would know him to see him today. I was that close.

By now the young sisters had followed Charles down to the spring, wondering what could possibly keep the boy so occupied. They too now pressed in upon the hunched figure seated by the spring.

----So how did it happen? Charles asked.

John hesitated, assessing Charles' age and ability to hear the details of war. He did not open any doors as he had with George earlier. He spoke as a reporter who had written a story.

----Well, you've heard tell of "bloody Shiloh". It is a right apt name.

The children were immediately spellbound. They could not resist a good story, especially a war story told by a real hero. John had not spoken of his injury at Pittsburgh Landing, as most of his comrades called the battle, and he did not consider himself much of a storyteller, but he seemed to warm to the moment. The horror of the two days of hard fighting had lost their sting as the years passed from that early April in '62. He told of the events as if he were an outside observer, seeing it all very clearly, but dispassionate.

----I can tell ya' what I rememba' of my own account, but I can't speak foa' many otha's. I rememba' the long march on Thursday and Friday befoa' the battle. We were plum wore out when we got to Corinth. Saturday was spent in some minor ski'mishes and some scoutin', and then came Sunday. We moved in on Pittsburgh Landing early on the mo'nin', about 9:00 AM. The orda' to charge was given by Colonel Deas, and foa'ward we went. The storm of musketry soon became deafening, so that had I been hit, thea' would have been no recognition otha' than the pain. But I remained lucky. Scores fell nea' me, but I was unha'med, so I moved foa'ward. The Colonel had moved out front to rally us, foa' the witherin' fia' had nearly stalled us out. I saw him look down at his hand and could see foa' myself the blood. He turned and continued to press foa'ward amidst the screamin' lead. Just in front of me I saw him get hit again. This time his ho'se was shot from unda' him. The animal stood erect and fea'less so nea' in front that I could have touched her. She took a ball that could have been mine. At the same instant, Colonel Deas was plucked by anotha' ball at his hip and one at his right a'm. He and his magnificent ho'se crashed to the ground befoa' me. The colo' beara' stopped, his flag in no direction tilted. I stooped to attend to oua' leada', and he grabbed me by the colla' and said to me, "I'm all right, private. Don't let 'em break. You hea'? Don't let the colo's touch the ground. This day is oua's!" So, naturally, bein' admonished by the Colonel himself, I grabbed hold of the arm of the offica' beside me as he clutched the flag and togetha' we made a death march into the Yanks. At fi'st I thought the memba's of the colo' guard would orda' me back into rank, but they had seen the Colonel talkin' to me and figur'd I had orda's. So anyway, I pressed foa'ward with the brave soldia's in charge of the colo's. I didn't know if anyone was behind me and I didn't care. I was gonna' pass into glory. Then to my complete joy, I heard a wild shout and the blue boys in front began to run. And did they eva' run. We had mostly surprised them and they had left thea' camps with fia's still burnin' and coffee cookin'. I couldn't help noticin' as I chased 'em that they had all the comfo'ts of home in camp. There were mattresses, featha' beds, quilts, stoves and everything in thea' tents. And the food! We had to halt the chase, so many stopped to plunda'. Can't blame 'em much. All we had to eat was pork fat and pickled beef. So that was a grand day foa' the glorious 22nd, and foa' yoa' brotha's. The next was as terrible as the fi'st was grand.

Come Monday the Yanks was not yet gone from the field entirely, although pressed back seve'ely and smartin' from thea' loss. As I came to find out lata', it was General Buell's A'my of the Ohio that arrived on scene with about 40,000 men to reinforce. We had no reinforcements and braced to fight again a second day. Across the way we could make out the Hessians, 10,000 strong. We attacked with the 90 we had left in the 22nd. It was a gallant and deadly affai'. I had barely begun my march into the opposin' lines when I felt a tug at my coat nea' my shoulda'. At fi'st I thought it was square through my heart, but when I crumpled to the ground I scrambled to find the wound and discovered it was through my chest neara' the shoulda'. The blood kind of oozed on out, and for a moment I just watched it. Then figurin' I better stop the bleedin', I tore off a piece of my shirt and stuffed it in the wound. I had some of Pa's whiskey in a flask just foa' such an occasion and drank it generously. I was a little weak from the loss of blood, so I just sat and waited for the events to unfold. Shua' enough some cheea's rose up from the field. We had taken some batteries. Unfortunately the rest of the a'my had not faired as well and we were forced to relinquish oua' positions lata'. But foa' the time I looked about at the shatte'ed remains of those left to writhe in death's grip on the field. I could make out a crowd gathered around one wounded and knew of course he must be an offica'. It was our brigade commander, General Gladden. He had an arm picked clean from his body in the same volley, I believe, that had felled me. It turns out that Colonel Adams got a sevea' shot to the head and Major Armistead was wounded mortally with grapeshot through the bowel. As for me, I lingered on the battlefield foa' several hours unable to muster strength to move from loss of blood. Finally, I was assisted from the field and taken to the hospital. That's whea' they pushed the silk through the hole to clean it out. I'll remember that foa' a while. I won't soon forget the many friends I lost that day, eitha'. I had to listen to 'em die while I waited foa' my own fate that day.

John had almost forgotten he was talking to the young ones. He lowered his vision to the place where they stood agape. He had become lost in the recollection and was beginning to recount the horrors without editing the facts that would give the impressionable listeners some very nasty dreams. He backed away from the hard memories.

----So I got a forty day furlow and came on home foa' a little while and rejoined the outfit in Kentucky no wo'se foa' the wea'. It was that wound at Chickamauga that really laid me up.

Charles shouted out abruptly.

----Tell us Johnny! Tell us about the battle!

The others chimed in, apparently satisfied with his telling of Shiloh. The memory of Chickamauga, and the recounting of it with George occurred to him.

----Anotha' day kids. Anotha' day.

They all went away wanting for more and mumbling a bit to themselves. John was left again to his thoughts. He had figured that on the morrow he would find out a little about his adversary, Stephen Pratt. Any man who avoided combat with men at arms and instead waged war on negroes and women was clearly without honor, and it could be expected that he would be capable of anything. Some things did not add up. If the dying man he obtained a confession from was telling the truth,

130

Pratt had ordered an attack on Job and on Sophie. Yet the city boy gave every intention that he had plans to marry her. Maybe this was an act of vengeance. Or maybe it was her father Pratt had aught against. By destroying a man's property and harming his family, one could achieve an ultimate revenge. Taking Mr. Croft's life would not be as sweet as wrecking his family if one were seeking some kind of pay back. Whatever it was, John knew he would protect Sophie at any cost. Asking her a few questions might give him the answers he needed , but he determined not to trouble her with this disturbing news, especially given the condition of her father. He would set out for Montgomery tomorrow morning. There he could ask some old friends about one Stephen Pratt whom he had no doubt was very much in the public eye. John doubted there would be many secrets among the town folk. And they were always willing to tell what they knew, or thought they knew.

John rose from his seat by the spring satisfied with his plan. He would assist the others with the weeding of the corn, and then ready himself for the midnight vigil being held for Job. In the periphery of his vision he saw a rider snaking along the path that led from Owl's Hollow Road. It looked to be a single rider , but John did not want to take chances. He quickly snatched his gun from the side of the springhouse and awaited the interloper. He did not intend to be another victim of angry blue troops hell bent on revenge. As he neared, John saw that the man was riding cautiously, obviously unfamiliar with the area. He was thin, poorly but neatly dressed, and searching. He spotted John and rode in his direction. John held his gun in a visible but non-threatening manner across his chest, barrel skyward.

The rider halted his winded and spattered horse at a short distance.

----Are you John Huff?

The man looked vaguely familiar and it was not until he saw the smooth, hairless skin on his neck and arms, and the oozing gauze that he knew who he was.

----I am. I'm very glad to see you well.

John eased the gun to his side and placed it against the earth bank behind him.

The stranger unseated himself and stood before John, offering his hand. There were tears welling in his eyes and he could barely speak through the tide of emotions that overwhelmed him.

----I am very grateful that you saved my life. My wife and children send thea' thanks and thea' regret that they could not come themselves.

----So yoa' not soa' that I hit ya'?

The quiet gentleman smiled and shook his head, then paused. He had become suddenly serious.

----Mr. Huff, I'm hea' to thank you and hopefully to retu'n the fava'.

John looked puzzled. The speaker got quickly to the answer.

----I took a job as waita' on the Laura Moore the day afta' the accident. I was se'vin' some fancy dressed dandy when he decided to insult me. He was seated with a pretty lady who had a very conce'ned look, so I thought I might listen to see what was of interest. A bad habit I know, but it relieves some of the monotony of the work. Anyway, I had my back to the couple when I heard yoa' name mentioned. I had asked, as soon as I could talk afta' the fia', who had pulled me from the wata'. Someone gave me yoa' name. I had hoped to

132

thank you some day. So naturally, I listened moa' ca'efully.

There was some hesitation before the waiter delivered what he hoped would be the climactic words.

----She called him Stephen. Does the name mean anything to you?

The hairs prickled on John's neck.

----Oh yes, go on.

----I couldn't catch it all, but I do know that you could be in danga'. He is afta' some land and he believes that you ah' an obstacle. He o'dered an attack on a young lady and he hopes that it will sca'e her and her fatha' into sellin' it to him.

----You've been very helpful. I would say we ah' even.

The man looked relieved as though he had made a final payment on a very large debt.

----Do you know the girl's name he was with?

----I believe he called her Anna. I wish I knew moa', but that was all I could gatha'

He spoke the last words as he mounted the horse and turned once more to face John.

----Good luck and thank you.

----It was my pleazha'. God's speed.

Sometimes, John thought, fate is uncommonly generous. And he felt that just now. He considered the timely news divine intervention, coming to aid the side of both love and justice. This would save him a trip to Montgomery. Now what to do with the information. He still could not trouble Sophie with it, and the Yankee military law would not necessarily be concerned with his accusations. And even his fellow members of the Circle might be hesitant to act on a man of wealth and prominence. He would certainly have to think on this one. And so it was for the land. Yes, that made more sense. He is in love with another and greed is his mistress. But love and greed are not very good bedfellows. They are akin to love and honor. Too often you must choose between one or the other. He wants the woman of his choice and the land of his dreams. He lacks the moral reasoning to realize he cannot justly have them both.

John believed he had it mostly figured out. War had among other things made him keenly aware of the heart of men. He had seen the best of the human heart, but he had also witnessed the worst. He was not so naive as when he had first left the farm in 1861. He had seen plenty of men just like Stephen who had nothing to check their conscience. They allowed their passions for whatever the vic e may be to run amuck in their lives and eventually own them. So it was, he guessed, with Stephen. John had tried all his life to live under the ever-present shadow of God, family, honor and society. And although he was not blameless, he had faired well, he believed, in the eyes of God and men. And then there was the killing. It was difficult to justify the killing. One who has lived a moderate and moral existence should never have to deal with justifying murder. Still, he had read his Old Testament enough to realize that God was a God war. And in the end He will be a God of war again. Done. He could live with the killing as part of God's plan. He believed sincerely that he would escape God's judgement and his wrath. He had played according to the rules of war. There was honor in fighting fair and in fighting hard. Just as certainly though, John concluded that Stephen Pratt would not escape God's justice. There was nothing honorable in his coveting of the Croft plantation or his taking of innocent lives. In this life or the next, he was certain Stephen Pratt would pay. And if God willed, it would be at John's own hand.

And so, as John wound his way back to his homestead, his thoughts turned from the unpleasant to the sublime. When this mess with Stephen was over he could cultivate his relationship with Sophie. He had assumed that her willingness to kiss him was a sure sign of her affections. Maybe he was being presumptuous. What if even now she was racked with regret? The smug confidence that comforted him just a short time ago appeared to fade in direct relation to the time removed from when he kissed her last, so that by this evening he might wonder if she really cared for him at all. He could hardly wait for the darkness to come. And strange as it was he found himself counting the moments until he could attend a funeral that he very much looked forward to. No disrespect to Job intended. He rather hoped Job approved. Something about burying a man creates a sacred bond. John spoke aloud as he walked, asking for the beloved servant's blessing. In his mind's eye he could see the gray bearded face, wool cap and nod of consent. He hoped Sophie's father would approve of him courting his daughter as readily. He feared he hoped for too much.

Chapter Twelve

Sophie felt as though her emotions were a tangible thing. It was as if they were thrown upon a Medieval torture rack and stretched beyond endurance. She was taken in a matter of moments from the heights of joy to the despair of sorrow and lingering death. Papa was unable to raise himself up from his bed. Sophie, Louisa, and Aunt Molly had held a constant vigil by his side from the moment she had returned from the orchard. The faithful old mammy never seemed to lose concentration on the old man. She read every sigh, heard ever raspy breath, and moved swiftly to remedy the anomaly. The concern was evident in the lines of her face which reflected her wisdom and experience with such matters. Aunt Molly had doctored Sophie herself when she was fevered and it was feared she would be lost. The sturdy old African had nursed her slowly and lovingly back to complete health. Sophie was confident that if her father could be helped, then Aunt Molly would be his best hope. Molly sent Sophie to get some rest at about eight o' clock in the evening. She had been resting fitfully since then. It was 11:30, and John would be along very soon to attend the midnight burial of Job.

She hadn't had time to think much about what had happened earlier with John. It was quite a shocking turn of events. He had kissed her at a most unusual moment and she had so willingly submitted to the advance. She hoped sincerely that he did not think ill of her for yielding so quickly. But the moment had come so abruptly and with so little warning that she did not have a chance to brace herself. And she had wanted so badly for it to happen. She wondered what he was thinking right now. Had he regretted it? It was like knocking apples out of a tree that sits close to a house. You want the apple so much that you don't notice how close the window is. As soon as you let go of the offending object, you question if you made a mistake. And then, sure enough, you break the window. Then the prize, even though you got it, maybe, doesn't seem so sweet. Well, she had found the intimate moment very sweet. She now hoped that John didn't feel like he had broken a window. She would know by his actions tonight. And if it turned out that he apologized for what he believed was a mistake, well then it would just be another turning of the rack stretching her beyond what she could bare. And then would come the thumb screw. Her father would die and she and her sisters and whatever of the servants wished to go would leave this place. With John by her side she believed that she could overcome it all. She liked him very much, yet she was uncertain if she loved him. But she knew that she *could* love him, and in that there was hope.

A knock at her door broke her pensive state. Aunt Molly's soft voice accompanied the staccato rap of her weathered knuckles on the hard wood.

----Miz' Sophie, can I be seein' ya fo' a moment, ma'am?

Sophie's heart raced with the anticipation of the bad news. She rushed to the door unable to determine from Molly's words if the urgency was for the worst. She opened the door to the weary looking Molly who slurred some as she spoke, due to her lack of rest and the constant care she was providing. Her face provided no more clues. When at last she spoke, Sophie's eyes widened with anticipation. She braced herself for the words that she dreaded most of all. But they were not yet to come. Aunt Molly mustered a feeble smile.

----Marse Croft is doin' betta'. His coughin' spells ah' nea' done and he is sittin' up in bed. He can't yet get up, but I thought you'd wants to know.

----Thank you, Molly, I knew if he could be made to feel betta', it would be you who could manage it. Get some rest now. I'll have Sadie sit with Papa a while.

----If it's all the same to you Ma'am, I'll just res' in Marse Croft's room.

Molly bowed her head and with heavy steps returned to the sick man's chamber to keep watch for the one who counts men's every heartbeat and send him unhappily away. Sophie in the meantime had a moment's reprieve from the emotional struggle that had gripped her. She might have a moment to think on such trivial things as love and happiness. It was nearly midnight and John would be along soon. What does one wear at such an event. It had been some time since she had attended a negroe funeral. The family always paid respects but did not always participate in the evening ritual. Something black would not be difficult to find. During the war it seemed sometimes that black was all that one could wear. She searched her wardrobe and instead lighted upon a black shawl she could throw over what she was wearing. She needed to see Papa before she left, but she did not want to startle him by walking into his room shrouded in black. So she decided on the shawl. She quickly set about making herself presentable for the evening. It took only a moment to pin her hair neatly back over her ears and wash her face. Sophie turned the corner of the hallway and into her father's room. He was asleep. She stepped to his bed, leaned over him, and kissed his forehead. She then turned and rushed out the door and down the stairs where Quinton was waiting. He stood erect, hands folded in front and draped completely in black. His face was void of expression.

----You ready, Miz' Sophie?

----Have you hea'd yet from Mr. Huff, Quinton?

----No, ma'am.

Sophie reached the bottom stair and before she could turn, heard her name called out from the back of the house. It was Jack Arp.

----Sophie, miss, I need to speak to ya' on somethin' ratha' urgent, if you could.

He was speaking to her through the entrance of the door to the rear of the house.

----Whateva' it is will have to wait, Jack.

She shouted the words in his general direction while turning back to the front of the house.

----It couldn't be any moa' urgent than a dozen otha' problems that ah' about.

Her last words trailed away as she stepped out onto the front piazza. She peered into the dark, looking for some sign of John. He was riding hard and she could now recognize his form from a distance even in the night. That should mean something. Familiarity. He was through the alley and past the garden, stopping just in front of her. In the dim light she tried to read his face. He didn't look like one who had broken a window. He dismounted nimbly from the marvelous horse, red-brown with a white bib. Wrapping the reins 'round a

white porch post he said cheerily, "Evening, Sophie".
She thought it a good sign.

----Oa' should I say good mo'nin'?

It was just after midnight. The negroes had assembled out back and had begun the low, earthy hum of the spirituals they summoned up from deep in their mournful souls. His tone quickly turned serious.

----How is yoa' fatha'?

Sophie lowered her gaze.

----He is very sick, John. He has shown improvement, though, since earlia' today. We had thought he might slip from us.

----I'll pray foa' his speedy recovery.

----I believe prayin' is in orda'.

There was then an awkward silence as each was unsure how to proceed without some reference to the moment that had created a bridge for their mutual crossing. Sophie, being the better master of language and quicker of wit than the deliberate John, interjected, hoping to restore some ease. Quinton, who had been standing in the doorway, realized the discomfort and took his que to step back inside and close the door. Sophie turned her head to the side and spoke to John.

----I ratha' expected you might not arrive this evening.

John looked surprised.

----Why wouldn't I?

----Well, I thought maybe you felt like you made a mistake, you know, kissing me like you did.

----A mistake? If I offended you, Sophie...

----Oh, no. I just wasn't shua' how you felt. It happened so fast.

John smiled with the assurance that she indeed was accepting of him and of his affections. He reached his hand to both of Sophie's and grasped them firmly as if securing a bond. She turned toward him.

----It really wasn't that fast. I had pictured that moment a hundred times. It seemed like to me, well, the hundred and fi'st.

----Only a hundred?

She pouted in mock disappointment. John took her arm in his and together they walked to the "quarters". Sophie felt relief, joy, and something like a rush of excitement surge through her. She was overwhelmed by the power of spoken affection. He desired her and it was intoxicating. Suddenly her future seemed brighter. And she knew that it was John.

As they turned the corner of the front portico they ran headlong into a rushing Jack Arp. The sudden movement startled them all to attention. Jack stood straight up and tugged at the bottom of his ill-fitting jacket, adjusted his hat. He looked askance at John. Sophie couldn't help but notice the conscious effort made by Jack to avoid him. It seemed that John was puzzled by it also. Weren't they as of yesterday conspiring together?

Sophie made a mental connection between Jack's behavior and the immediacy with which he asked to speak to her.

----Why, Jack. You really should not be in such a hurry. You're beginning to act like a northerna', always rushin' about. Did you need to speak to me?

Jack fidgeted, paused, and looked again furtively at the silent John. He exhaled an exasperated sigh.

----No ma'am, I guess I'll just talk to ya' later.

He bowed, tipped his hat, and disappeared into the darkness.

If she had any doubt it was now gone. The tension was about John. Sophie remembered that just the other day Jack was peering in the window at her. And he was very cold around John this afternoon. Could he possibly be jealous? She was amused at the idea of it. She had never noticed any unusual attention from him.

As the couple walked again arm in arm the sounds of the negroe spirituals grew more distinct. The words of a favorite hymn were discernible Sophie had heard i so often that she knew the words and sang along, "Jesus, Savior of my Soul". A throng of singing servants gathered 'round the narrow pine box made by negroe craftsman. Torches were burning dimly, casting pulsating shadows on the wooden shroud. Black, glistening faces shone wet with tears. Sophie and John stepped close. The coffin bearers, in the midst of the singing, took their positions at each of the four corners. Silas and Quinton stood at the front, while Tobias and Ben, the blacksmith, manned the rear corners. The four men hoisted the box to their shoulders and began to step in unison, accompanied by the mourners and their yellow-orange light. The rest, with Sophie and John followed close behind as the solemn procession snaked along the trodden path to the Croft cemetery for the servants. The song turned to a well known funeral dirge.

Hark from the tomb a mournful sound;
Mine ears attend a cry
Ye living men come view the ground
Where you must shortly lie.

When they reached the appropriated hole in the ground both movement and singing came to an abrupt stop. The sweetly scented pine box was lowered carefully into the depression as the onlookers watched it disappear away from the flickering light. Quinton stepped to the head of the narrow chasm just behind a wooden cross that bore the scrawled words:

Job Croft
Faithful Servant
Faithful Friend

Quinton opened the Bible but did not bother to read it. His deep bass voice echoed into the stillness of the very new morning.

----We are hea' today fo' oua' friend Job.

A chorus of "amens" and "yesses" greeted the words along with other utterances of affirmation.

----He was a good man. He was an honest man. He was a man full of the joy of oua' Lo'ad. Job worked ha'd. And not one hea' eva' heard him complain. He left one day lookin' foa' land. And he found the promised land. He hoped for a little shack on the land. And he got a mansion.

By now the assemblage of Africans was half full of grief and half full of rejoicing at the pleasant image of Job wandering the halls of a greathouse beyond description. There was a strange cacophony of sound in the air, some laughing, some weeping, others praying aloud. To Sophie's astonishment, John stepped to the place where Quinton was at the head of the grave. The crowd fell silent. John reached into his pocket and

143

withdrew a crumpled piece of paper. With the paper still in his hand he reached up and took off his slouch hat putting it beneath his immobile arm. His voice was soft and the listeners had to strain to hear.

----As you prob'ly know, I am the one who found Job on the road the otha' day. You prob'ly know, too, that I buried him on some adjoining land. I would like to sha'e what I said as I stood as I do hea' now, ova' his grave. I didn't know him well, but from what I saw I believe he was indeed a good man, no betta' from what I hea', could be found eitha' negroe oa' white. I prayed that his crops be plentiful and that the angels themselves would tend his fields. This letta' I hold in my hands is an invite from his brotha' to come live in Mississippi whea' he would be given his own fa'm. He clutched it in his hands whea' he fell that day. He died with a promise in his hand and hope in his heart. May we all cling to a hope in this very troubled time, that will see us to betta' days.

There were many nods and affirmations when John had finished. He made his way back to Sophie's side and the funeral concluded with more singing and the piling of dirt. The living returned along the way they had come. John and Sophie paused in the ebony night beside the corn crib. All roads from the plantation lead there, corn being such a vital crop. Soon it would be filled and overflowing with the useful food. John found two carrying baskets, turned them over one in front of the other, and invited Sophie to sit. She eased herself onto one of the crates and John sat astride, directly across. He put his hands on her knees and looked into her eyes. He seemed very serious.

----Sophie, I've gotta' tell ya' honestly. From the moment I saw you the otha' day, I knew I wanted to be whea' you were. In fact, as I look ova' the days since I've been home, the most meaningful moments have been spent with you. I'm not gonna' ask foa' any moa' than that just now. Can we spend moa' time togetha'?

Sophie smiled sweetly and leaned in close. She had thought for a moment he was going to surprise her again with a sudden and unexpected proposal.

----I assumed that when you kissed me, you had intended that we might be getting to know each otha' a bit moa'. Otha'wise, what kind of girl would I be?

John looked poised to defend himself and his intentions. He quickly realized Sophie was being playful. She rose and taking his hand led him to the front piazza where the night had begun. When she got to the door she stood beneath the fantail and turned to John once again.

----Thanks foa' coming, John. It is very late and I need to check on Papa. Will I see you tomorrow?

----You will see me today.

Sophie had forgotten the hour. It was she this time who leaned over and kissed him tenderly on his cheek.

----Good night, Sophie

John turned and with unexpected agility leaped upon the horse and sped away down the empty road. She watched until he was gone and out of sight.

She would go and see about her father. The fear that should accompany her was not there. She felt a courage she had not felt before. If he had worsened in the last hour she simply would take care of him. And John would be back soon. She drew comfort from his presence. It was easy to want him near all the time. She had been leaning against one of the bulky white columns and wheeled around to go inside. And she nearly ran into him again. Jack had emerged with perfect stealth and was now inches form her. He was standing so close that she stepped back, uncomfortable with the distance. She could not form any words.

----Miss Sophie. I need to speak to ya' now.

----Jack, it's ha'dly the time. Papa is ill, and it is very late. What is it that can not wait?

She was afraid of him in this moment. The skulking, following, strange looks, and now the persistent need to speak to her.

----It's about John, Ma'am.

----What about John?

----I'm afraid he may not be what he seems. I'm sorry to tell ya' 'cause I know yoa' fond of him.

She was beginning to be alarmed. Her fear of Jack became secondary to her fear of the words that might follow. He continued. He told a story of clandestine meetings. Sophie had ventured into one of them the night of the barbecue. He told of riding into the hollow and of chasing the renegades. He slowed as he told about John standing over one of the dying outlaws.

----This is the part that concerns me, Miss Sophie. He positioned himself away from the rest of us, I think foa' a reason. I believe he wanted all of 'em dead. What I'm tryin' to say is I think he was behind yoa' assault.

Sophie was dumbfounded. There must be some mistake. For what possible reason? She stared at him but said nothing. He explained.

----All the otha's were dead and when I came to the top of a hill I saw John standing ova' the last of the villains. I yelled to John to spare him 'cause he was the only one left to talk. I was close enough I could read the man's lips. He was saying, "help me". As I neared I could see he was talkin' moa'. John did nothin'. He watched him die. I asked him if the man said anything and John said that he hadn't. When I saw John he had his gun raised and the trigger cocked.

Jack paused trying to gage Sophie's reaction. She bade him continue.

----Thea' is moa'. Maybe you didn't know, but Mr. William Huff made it known that he would send his sons to fight in the war, but he would see to it if they came back they would have somethin' to come back to. He invested heavily in Union enterprises. It is common knowledge that he is lookin' to buy up prope'ty to extend his holdings. Yoa' prope'ty is the only one separating him form direct access to the riva'. You probably didn't know either that John has taken ova' the business of the farm oa' that the railroad proposal that ran the railroad through Huff's Gap has been postponed. It all kind of makes sense, Sophie. Add to it that Owl's hollow borders the Huff's property and that the Huffs have distilleries at the edge of the hollow, well, it seems very likely.

Sophie's heart sank. She had a sudden feeling of nausea. It wasn't damning evidence, but it did make sense. She wanted to object and call the accusation ridiculous. But she did not want to be someone whose judgment was clouded because of romantic interest. She would not be anyone's fool. She had planned to find answers for herself, but so much had been going on she hadn't yet had the chance. A change came over Sophie very suddenly. She straightened up her back. She became instantly resolute. She had been pushed to the wall and she was determined to fight back. It occurred to her just then that she had been acting rather foolishly. She had been allowing herself to be tossed about by her emotions. Despair, love, worry, would not rule her existence, no. Where was the strength she had when her mother was ill and the war was raging? Where was the Sophie who had fended off the Union army? She willed her mind to focus.

----How is it that you know these things, Jack?

----Yoa' daddy had me keep watch of you while he was away. When he heard what happened on the road he asked me to continue. I saw you at the party with John, and I knew you were takin' to him.

----That explains then how he knew. I had wondered.

----I am very sorry, Miss Sophie. We all ah' just lookin' out foa' you.

----That is all very well, Jack, but may I suggest that you direct yoa' energy elsewhea'. I will not need coddled any longa'. I will deal with Mr. Huff myself as I see fit. And as foa' this place you may tell all the se'vants thea' need not be any conce'n foa' them. We will all prospa' hea'. If that is all, Jack...

----Yes, ma'am.

He turned and made his way back to the quarters. Sophie was left with a starry night and a bushel of questions. She was not sure who she could trust. It seemed to her that the servants were the most trustworthy folks she knew. Jack could be lying. But what would that serve him? Maybe he wanted the plantation. Maybe he wanted her.

She felt like a caged animal. Preservation for her and her family would have to be utmost in her mind. Her brush with love had been bittersweet at best. The possibility existed that John was in fact completely innocent and there must be some other reasonable explanation. She could not afford, however, to be mistaken. She had already invested too much. It was best to cut her losses now. She needed a plan. Standing, looking into the evening stars, Sophie decided very quickly what needed to be done. A whippoorwill chimed its sad lament to the boundless night sky. She became lost in its sonorous melody. The front door opened with such force that Sophie could feel the vacuum it created. There stood Aunt Molly with a look like John might have carried into his first battle.

Chapter Thirteen

Stephen would not leave matters to chance. He had received word late last night that Mr.Croft was bed ridden. Here was an opportunity. He closed his eyes and he could almost see it all play out. He would arrive at the old man's bedside before his dying breath. David Croft would call in his eldest daughter and Stephen himself. He would take their hands and join them together and ask him to take care of Sophie, her sisters and the plantation. And all of it would be his. He was certain Sophie would not deny her father's dying wish. He would catch them both at a weak moment. Anna, unfortunately, would be sacrificed to prosperity. She said she would be waiting at the ferry crossing for him after he delivered the news to Sophie that he would not marry her. Poor Anna had no idea what was about to happen. She would take it hard, but she would recover quickly. A woman had to. To pine away the days would leave one a bitter spinster--the equivalent of social death. But for himself, he would leave a legacy of wealth and reputation for the generations that would follow him. And until then he would lead the life of a planter--a life of ease. He would have servants and land and leisure. He would hunt fox in the woods on crisp mornings and entertain guests to many-coursed meals in the evenings.

Stephen stood in the parlor of his home in front of a large looking glass. He picked up his planter's hat and placed it ceremoniously on his head. It was broad-brimmed, straw- colored and circular. He studied himself from various angles and being satisfied with his appearance, stepped outside to his waiting horse. The town made him feel confined. He didn't like the closeness of the buildings or the noise in the streets. He wanted to look out upon his cultivated fields and to open the front door to the smells of the countryside. He put his foot in a stirrup and leaped aboard to begin his ride back to Turkeytown, his dream, and his destiny.

And so it was that John woke on this morning of August the 20th, 1865. Looking out the window of the old salt box house jammed with the living, breathing souls that meant everything to him, he assessed the last few days. In this place he considered something like a treasure-chest full of his most precious possessions, there was one jewel missing---the crown jewel, and he had found it so close to home in the person of Sophie. And although the road to his happiness with her seemed to be wide open, there were the barriers that could prove insurmountable. He was glad he had not mentioned to Sophie what he had learned about Stephen. He knew when he did tell her that it would be a hard blow for sure. And he would have to tell her. Everything. He did not want to chance losing her like he almost had when he neglected to tell her of Job. And she had proved to be much stronger than he could have guessed. He should not underestimate her again. Still, he must choose the right time.

The sun was rising and the house began to stir. Today they would plant the black-eyed peas in the rows between the corn. This would help secure the root systems of the corn and prevent the heavy winds that come in the fall from uprooting the crop. To say nothing of the goodness of the black-eyed peas themselves.

Mother was up early and surprised to see that John had usurped her position as first riser this glorious morning.

----Mo'nin' John. Yoa' up earlia' than usual.

----Mo'nin' to you, Ma. I've a lot to think on and my mind is most clea' early on in the day.

----You ah' so much like yoa' fatha'. Anything I can help with?

----No, just a few things I have to work out on my own.

She scratched at the damned fleas that were such a pestilence. The bedding was never rid of them and they harassed the evening inhabitants unmercifully. The scratching was loud enough to be audible until Georgia's voice drowned it out. Georgia, being almost eight was very spry and often up just after her mother. She was a cute, wild-haired little thing and John was quite fond of her. She reminded him very much of Sophie at that age. "She isn't bad", he would tell his mother,"she is just spirited". He often defended her even when she had been naughty. Like the time she washed the cat with turpentine so as to get her real clean. The cat lost its hair and died, and mother was livid. John explained that Georgia had watched her mother clean, and was just "imitatin'". It tempered her anger a bit.

----Johnny!, Johnny!, will you walk me into Death's Shade Hollow today? You promised.

The depression that formed between the ridge that divided the close of the apex and the ridge behind the house was precipitous and thickly wooded. It was given the name Death's Shade by the Cherokee possibly because the ridges and trees allowed little light to penetrate, but also because of its steep terrain, prohibiting all but spirits from regular travel. The children were quite afraid to venture into the "other" hollow even though it was far less threatening than Owl's Hollow with the riffraff that dwelled there. John was non-committal.

----I've got some things to do today, Georgia, maybe tomorrow, eh?

----Shua', Johnny. You goin' to see Soo-phi?

She dragged out the name in the way that only children can, and gave a stern look to show her disappointment. John smiled, amused at her childishness.

----I suppose I will, Georgia. That all right with you?

----I guess. I don't know her that well, though.

By now the rest of the house was up. Not that there was much of a choice. Brother George had roused himself and was listening with interest to John's discussion with Georgia. He interjected.

----How 'bout my own brotha' steelin' my gi'lfriend.

John laughed at what he thought was an attempt at humor. Only George was not smiling. He didn't seem angry, he just seemed serious.

----Well, had I known George...

----Ah well, it's all right. If I had to lose her I suppose its betta' to have lost out to kin.

This time he did smile, but it did make John wonder how much truth was in George's jesting. After a short pause George amended his earlier statement.

----Fact is, if you weren't my big brotha' I might have to call ya' out to duel.

George continued with the light humor. John thought about what a spectacle it would be to see brothers duel over the want of a woman. He had heard of just such a thing. Two brothers in Tennessee had gotten into a fight at the dinner table. They dueled, one from each end of it, and one was killed. Duelling George would be a tough go. He had turned himself into an excellent marksman with a pistol which was a very unsure weapon beyond even twenty feet. Most Southern farmers were quite good with a rifle but few had ever bothered with a pistol. George took it up as a bit of a hobby. John's remarkable shot that struck the leg of the one outlaw was a bit of very good luck or divine intervention. He doubted he could strike a target again that way given thirty more attempts. It was no surprise to know that George had never been challenged in the dying art. Of course neither had he. But it had nothing to do with how good a shot either of them was. Gentlemen were more likely to engage in duels. They seemed to have more opportunities to offend each other. His father, William, had strived to break into the genteel class, but the Huffs were just outside it, not having quite enough land or any servants to associate on a level equal to, say, the Crofts. It was evident that class distinctions so carefully defined before the war were deteriorating rapidly, however. There were those, still, who would hold on to their Southern aristocracy with white-knuckled fists. To John it all mattered very little. He labeled what he called the "lead aristocracy". Those who could avoid the lead were the ruling class.

----Tarnation, John. I was just kiddin'. Why you lookin' so serious?

John didn't realize he had lapsed into such whimsy.

----I was thinkin' about whea' I might want to be buried if we dueled.

The family had a good laugh with the two oldest surviving veterans. William H. returned from the barn to the joyous noise of his happy children. He had not smiled much since the news of the death of his oldest son, but there appeared on his face something like the ghost of one on his thin lips. All the children greeted him warmly.

----Papa!

The ghost of a smile gave way to a very visible one. With children dripping from his sturdy limbs, he directed his words to John who was standing near a window now streaming with golden sunlight.

----You wo'kin' fields oa' women today, John.?

Everyone of age sniggered, and John stood looking a little embarrassed. George covered for him to save him even more embarrassment.

----John has business ova' the riva', today, Isn't that right, John?

----Oh, umh, yes, I did tell widow Marsh that I would buy a scaldin' pot from her. I thought I would get it this mo'nin'.

The Huff patriarch narrowed his eyes.

----Hmmm.

----So, uh, I'll be on my way.

John left rather abruptly amidst the stifled giggles of his loved ones. He slipped out to the barn, saddled his horse and bolted off to the Crofts. Sophie had said they could spend more time together. She didn't say how much. He was anxious to see her. He had been straight forward about his feelings and he was glad. He felt confident that their subsequent meetings would strengthen the chords that had tied them. He spurred the white-chested horse down Turkeytown Road and on toward Croft Plantation.

Stephen Pratt galloped his fine horse up to the white columned house. He dismounted and left the animal to the care of Tobias who had greeted the gentleman with a courteous bow. Stephen postured and brushed the humble servant aside with no reply. Tobias shook his head and watched the dandy from the city enter the already opened door without the slightest obeisance. He acted as if he owned the plantation. Stephen did not ask to see Sophie. He instead demanded to see Master Croft. Quinton tried to dissuade him, telling him his master was gravely ill and could entertain no one. Stephen would not be deterred. He moved quickly by Quinton and up the curved staircase. Molly rebuffed him at the top of the stairs and he continued undaunted to Master Croft's room, she following him step for step, pleading him to let the old man rest. Molly stopped at the entrance to his room and watch as Stephen Pratt stepped lively to the side of his sick bed.
----Master Croft, are you asleep?
The decrepit man lifted his heavy lids and strained to focus on the visitor who stood near.
----I heard of your condition, sir, and came right away. I am sorry to see you in poor health.

The old man could only nod.   Stephen proceeded to his business in a very uncustomary manner, wasting no time on formalities. A Southern gentleman never broached his business without first taking time to enjoy some casual conversation and to inquire about the condition of health and family.

----Forgive me sir for getting so quickly to business but I believe I can assuage some of your fears. I have come to ask for your daughter in marriage today.   I can promise that she will want for nothing for as long as I live. Her sisters will be welcome here as well as your servants who have been your charge for so many years. Will you allow me her hand?

Sophie's papa paused for a moment, straining to look deeply into the eyes of the man who wished to claim what he valued most in his life. But his vision was blurred. He could not read the intent or the sincerity of the man who leaned over his bed, and so he mouthed the word in a breathy voice,--"yes".

----Splendid. This is a joyous day.

Sophie burst into the room having been alarmed by Molly of Stephen's presence.   He was beaming.

----My darling, Sophie. You are just in time.

She moved swiftly to her father's side. Her papa took her hand in his trembling own and without uttering a word, placed it upon Stephen's exactly as the dandy had forseen it. Pratt himself was astonished at the accuracy of his vision. Stephen did the talking.

----It has been long in coming, Sophie, but I have asked your father for permission to make you my wife. As you can see, he has assented. And now it is in your own hands. Will you accept your father's wishes and mine? Sophie, will you marry me?

She looked first at her father whose dying eyes listened for reply. She looked over her shoulder at Molly who was standing at the door looking very grim as if she were attendant to Master Croft's funeral rather than a wedding proposal. And then to Stephen who stood very near, holding her hand in his. She noted that it felt very awkward, her hand in his, but it was not altogether painful. For one wistful moment though, she wished it were John's hand she was holding. And then she remembered her resolve. Before she could lose her nerve she made a very "smart" decision for Croft Plantation and the family name. It was one that was not based on feelings or selfish wants. It was a decision rooted in duty, responsibility, and prudence. And Sophie said, "yes".

Chapter Fourteen

The horse that Tobias was leading away looked vaguely familiar. He brought his own to a stop and dismounted spryly, feeling rather like a school boy. He bounded the front steps and raised the brass knocker. The door opened and there stood Quinton. The trusted servant was disturbed.

----Marse John, I'ze glad you hea' sir. That man Pratt iz up to no good, I knowz it.

Quinton had uncharacteristically slipped into his relaxed speech, showing his level of ease with John, and his excitability, roused by the action taking place in the house.

John's manner changed quickly and violently. He, like his father before him, was one very slow to anger. But when his latent temper surfaced, the results were violent confrontations that he had little control over. He scaled the steps two at a time and hurried to the open door of the senior Croft. He could make out the partial form of the black clad Molly not inside and yet not out. As he got closer, he could see her face which bore a pleading, helpless look. He turned sharply into the room brushing past her and slowing very little. What he saw stunned him into a frozen halt. Sophie stood by her father's bedside. Her hands were in Stephen's, and her father's were clasping both. His rage had turned quickly to shock. Sophie had turned and stared, expressionless. Stephen too had turned, and a

159

mock grin exposed his perfect teeth. He spoke through them with an air of arrogance.

----Ah, Mr. Huff. As a close family friend may I be the first to tell you the good news. It is now official. Sophie and I will be married within the month.

John's heart pounded fiercely. His head pivoted to search the eyes of Sophie who stood with her lovely face, stoic as stone. There was nothing in them that he recognized. Something had gone very wrong. Having shaken off his dismay, he again returned to the anger that had rushed to his brain with his flowing blood. His eyes were wide with fury as he reeled on Stephen who was still looking very smug and obviously relishing in his victory.

----I don't know what you have told Sophie, but I know what you have done.

John took two steps forward in the direction of Stephen who had suddenly relaxed the smirk that he was wearing. The veteran fighter spoke again in a threatening tone.

----And I will send you back to the snake pit that you came slitherin' from. You ah' a lia' and a cheat, and I will not allow you to make a mockery of this good family.

Stephen managed to remain calm. Sophie bore a puzzled look, apparently confused by John's words. The old man was motionless. Master Pratt, somewhat ruffled, spoke his retort. He was very deliberate.

----Sir, you have violated this celebratory moment. You have violated the home of my lady. And you have impugned my good name. I have no choice but to demand redress. I am sure being a gentleman you are familiar with the *code duello*. Two hours hence I will be avenged. I will expect you on the road just out front---war hero.

This time Sophie interjected.

----Both of you stop this nonsense at once. There will be no duel. It is a ba'baric practice and not fit for civilized people to engage in. What is wrong with the both of you? You ah' actin' like children. This is not a game.

John replied while still glaring at Stephen.

----It is too late foa' that, Sophie. The challenge has been made and I am bound to uphold it. The truth will be revealed in the test of a'ms.

John wheeled on his heels and left the room as he had come. He hurried down the stairs and out the door. He mounted the horse still tied to a front column and headed home. As he turned out onto Croft Ferry Road, he slowed his horse to a trot. He began to think on the whole surreal drama. It would be necessary to keep himself calm when dealing with Stephen. The city boy had outwitted him. He had turned Sophie against him and now stood a good chance of taking it all, including his own life. John knew he had little chance against Stephen in a duel. And no doubt Stephen knew it, too. The man avoided warfare and would not likely pick a fight if he wasn't certain he would win. He had given the dandy an opportunity to be rid of him and he seized it. Withdrawing was not an option. Honor dictated that he accept the challenge. He had gained too much to watch his family name be smeared by a liar and a murderer. Death would be preferable. He simply must win. He would have to send a ball right through Stephen's heart and send him back to hell where he belonged, and then he would tell Sophie everything. And she would listen. Maybe God would exact justice at his own hand. John knew that a victory for himself in a duel would be a miracle, indeed.

John entered the dusty lane that bent to and fro between tall hickories. The looming possibility of death sharpened his senses once again. And he decided that home never looked quite so good. Charles greeted him and took the horse by the reins. John dismounted by the walnut tree that grew very near the house, partially obstructing the window he had peered out this morning. It was afternoon and all able bodies were in the fields of corn. He could see most clearly the two hired hands in their colorful tiaras, Bess and Teela. Bess's little one, Dilsey, was down below at the barn stirring up the chickens along with Georgia, of course.

John looked up to the top of the walnut tree to the branch where he used to sit when he was just a boy. Warm memories flooded over him in torrents. There was a time when he was without a care. When he was just a young boy and there was no threat of war, he used to climb in the trees, fish and swim in the lovely Coosa river, and hunt deer in the hollows. Much in him had changed since then, but he still longed for those carefree days. The arm had changed some of it. The horrors of war had changed some more of it. Hunting ceased to excite him. He had seen too many torn bodies to enjoy the tearing of more. Even if they were animals made to be hunted. Maybe that's what heaven would be--- endless childhood summers without fear or care. Or terrible memories. He heard heavy breathing and approaching steps. George's lanky limbs were eating up ground as he was walking briskly and in a surprisingly short moment he was standing before him, panting.

----How goes it big brotha'?

----Well, since ya' asked, not real good George.

----What, Sophie not bein' agreeable?

----Moa' than that, George.... Say, if ya' had to duel a man who you knew was a dead-eye shot, how would ya' go about it?

George looked incredulous but answered nonetheless.

----Foa' shua' I would make him take the first shot. That would be the man's only chance. If he shot and missed than the dead-eye would have time to aim and fia' without worry of a return. Who's duelin''?

----Me, George.

----What! Why?

----Long story, George. Can ya' help me get ready?

----I don't suppose I could talk ya' outta' it.

John just looked at him.

----No, no, I didn't think so.---How long do we have?

----Two 'oua's

----Two 'oua's! I have neva' heard of such a thing! Thea' must be a mediata'. And what of a second foa' each man? You must decline based on a disrega'd foa' the rules of engagement.

----I cannot.

George groaned and sighed all at once obviously troubled by the whole situation.

----I am goin' to talk to Pa and the little ones befoa' I go. Can you get yoa' pistol and meet me back of the house in a few minutes?

----Shua', John. I can tell ya' though, I don't like this one bit.

John Calhoun Huff sauntered out to the fields of his home for what he believed could be his last time. He breathed in deeply the sweat smell of corn silk as a gentle breeze blew it to him. He walked into a row of corn fully to the top of his head and found, first, his mother. He startled her as he stepped in behind where she was stooped.

----Hello, Ma.

----Johnny, you sca'ed me. Pick yoa' row, son.

----I have one moa' matta' to tend to Ma, and then I'll be out hea' in the dirt with ya'.

He hoped the ill timing of his words was not an omen.

----So what brings you hea', then?

She spoke the words to the ground, working while she talked.

----Just came to say I love ya' Ma.

Now she stood and turned to look at him.

----I love you, too, Johnny. Yoa' not tryin' to get out of work ah' ya'? You used to do that when you were a little boy. You would walk ova' to me and say you just needed a hug. And it took you some time befoa' you got back to workin'.

----Not this time, Ma

He had planned to say good-bye to everyone without really raising any fuss, but he decided it would be too hard, and so he went to the house and slipped around back. As he walked he pictured them all still in the fields and getting word from a neighbor that their son was dead. What a terrible shame it would be to survive a war and die in a silly damn duel. But it didn't feel silly. Things had changed, sure, but defending one's name he figured would always come as natural.

George apparently had not returned yet. John was again drawn to the old tree. He stood beneath it and on an impulse he reached up with his good arm and pulled himself to the first large branch. He began to climb. It wasn't quite as easy as it had been when he was very young. Climbing, like swimming, was a bit harder these days. It seemed effortless when he had both arms working. He reached the large flat bough that used to be his special place. And he sat. He looked out into the open end of the property that carried the name Huff's Gap. They were the first whites to inhabit the area amidst the Cherokee. They had lived in harmony until the evacuation of all natives at the hands of the government called 'The Trail of Tears".

The tree was tall enough that he could see his family working between the rows of corn. George was nowhere to be seen. He remembered that the two of them had just discussed dueling earlier in the day. John wondered if God was giving him signs. He was just at a funeral the night before, and then there was the talk of dueling today. Maybe they were the same signs that soldiers got before they went into battle. Many knew that the particular battle would be their last. They gave away possessions and wrote letters when they hadn't before and more often than not, they died. John believed Warren had experienced the signs before his death. But he himself did not feel the dread of dying. Maybe that was the real sign. While his mind was engaged with thoughts of God, they turned to the temptation of Christ as he looked down at the ground below. Satan tempted the Lord to throw himself down. He was tempted himself to do the same. Only a vaporous thought. It was gone in a moment. He had lived through too much to give it all back. Falling dead at the hands of one such as Pratt, though, would be far more painful than dying gloriously in battle. But God was clear on the issue. No one should take his own life. It made him feel a little ungrateful for even allowing it to enter his brain. But life without Sophie was one without color. The maroon Jack-in-the-pulpit that he could see spotting the parallel ridges looked less brilliant, and the red sumac was without luster. He could have told Sophie the truth about Stephen even as she held tight his hand. But something stopped him. Evidently she had been told something about him that she could not live with. That could be the only explanation given their interactions over the last few days. And that is what troubled him. She had lost faith in him somewhere. The words of another had overshadowed her belief in him and his character. But maybe he was partly to blame. He had mislead her with respect to Job, and that one act could be the one that cast a shadow of doubt. He refused to believe that she had suddenly and unexpectedly fallen in love with Stephen, nor did he figure she uncharacteristically opted for the wealth that Stephen would bring to her family. So, he would light a candle and hope she would find her way back to him through the darkness of lies and uncertainty. John felt it was a better course than to heap upon her the evidence that she would have to weigh and then decide whether or not to believe him. He wanted her to believe in him because of who he was and not because he had to persuade her of his sincerity or his innocence. However, if he did not win this duel he may never have the chance. The candle would be snuffed out with his life and Sophie could never find her way to him. He simply had to win. If the ancient code were true, John must be the victor because he fought on the side of truth. But that is how he felt about the Southern cause and the South had lost. He

166

could not say with his beloved General Lee that the issue had been settled by God in combat. There must be something beyond truth that settles such issues. Maybe it was fate or justice. In either case he hoped they were on his side today.

John figured he had been thinking too much. It was time to do battle. He did have one advantage. Although he wasn't good with a pistol, he had been in a number of tough scrapes before. He had stood in front of a gun barrel and he knew what it was to be shot.

George's plan was a good one. Stephen could be unnerved with a weapon pointed at him, and it may alter his shot if John waited to pull the trigger. With his strategy set, he figured it was time to practice a few shots with George's gun. He climbed down the tree very cautiously and mused at the irony of it given his momentary thought of jumping.

He certainly wanted to live. And that is what made this time of facing death so much harder than during battle. He had lost his will then. Now, he had a reason to live. John dropped from the lowest branch landing on both feet with a thud. He straightened himself for a moment looking for George who should have been out by now. And that is when he felt it. A violent blow to the back of his head made his whole body buzz and everything went very soft and black. The last thing he remembered was crumpling to the ground in an unconscious heap.

Chapter Fifteen

It was all her fault. She should have known this could happen. Looking after one's own interests often means to the detriment of others. In order to protect herself and her family she had jeopardized John's life. She felt it now a poor tradeoff. Stephen had left promptly after John to find a non-partisan mediator to conduct the duel. He had first stopped a middle-aged white courier who had just arrived from the river with some hemp rope he delivered to the plantation. He declined on the basis that he had to get back to the steamship that was preparing to leave. Since there were no other gentleman present, Stephen had told Sophie, Jack would have to do. He went to school him in the rules for the gentleman's duel. She was left to fret over her choices. She knew John well enough to realize that he would not stand idly by and allow her to marry Stephen without a fight. But she never would have guessed a duel would be the result. Dueling had been condemned over the last ten years by the clergy and even by the gentlemanly public. It did not completely eradicate the practice, but duels had declined markedly over the years. Sophie remembered that Stephen's father had engaged in several and emerged the victor in all three. Only one of the other men had been killed, but both were severely wounded. She feared for John because Mr. Pratt had seen to it that Stephen was an expert marksman. Having dueled himself and knowing that Stephen would be challenged because of his failure to join the Confederate army, his father had trained him as an expert marksman. She doubted there would have been a challenge, otherwise. Stephen had engaged in one duel that she knew of and the result was the death of the opponent. Stephen rarely missed. Sophie was frantic. She had made a dreadful mistake and there was now no stopping the events she had set in motion. When she thought of the man she had just pledged her life to, she became sick. He was duplicitous and self-serving. He knew John was not a man accustomed to the use of a pistol. Stephen would take his life and show no remorse. What kind of a man would consent to do such a thing?

She raised herself up from her bed where she had collapsed earlier and went to the back piazza. She could see Stephen there in his planter's hat talking to Jack. Jack kept nodding his head as if he understood his task. Once, Stephen looked up and saw her. He went directly back to his explaining without acknowledging her. Her heart sank to see him. What had she been thinking? Last night had put her in an awful state. The accusations by Jack and then the sudden appearance of Molly with the word that her father had lapsed into unconsciousness had affected her thinking. Now it was a matter of life and death. She must think clearly. Stephen had done something that had John very upset. Being one slow to anger, John would not have flung down an accusation without being certain of its truth. And she bet Stephen knew it, too. There was no question who she would believe. The servants didn't need to tell her that. She would confront Stephen. But that would not stop the duel. That had to be her focus. She must stop it. John had told her that night by the fire that she may have to trade a life for a life. She was willing to do it. And it gave her an idea.

Molly, laboring, walked out onto the piazza not bothering to ask permission.

----What in da' Lord's good name wuz ya' thinkin' Miz' Sophie. I ra'zed ya' wif mo' sense 'din 'dat. If y'uz tryin' to help us poor negro'z out, 'den you canz fo'get it. We don't stay hea' fo' 'da land, no ma'am. We stay in spite of it.

----I know, Molly, and I will fix it.

----Pa'don me, but y'uz fixed enuf.

----Yes, I know, but I can't let him kill John. And he will, if this duel is not stopped.

----Now you stay outs' it. 'Dis is man's biznss now.

Sophie turned to the bronze colored clock on her wall. It was ten minutes to the hour, and the dreaded duel.

----Molly, I must go. Keep Louisa inside.

Sophie scaled the stairs very quickly and rushed to the door. Quinton was standing with his back to her speaking to someone on the other side. Thinking it may be John, she moved more quickly. As Sophie neared the door, in stepped a delicate woman in a yellow ruffled dress, blonde hair, very green eyes, and fair skin which she was instantly envious of. The lady folded her parasol as she took two steps inside. The woman looked uncomfortable as if her corset had been drawn too tight. Quinton explained briefly.

----I told da' lady it was a very bad time for he' to call. But she said it was u'gent.

The woman did not wait for further explanation. She looked to be very nearly in tears.

----You must hea' me out, please.

----Hospitality is not foa'gotten hea' even in times of crises, of which thea' is one now, even at this moment. Foa'give my askin', but can you be brief?

A crowd had gathered at the front. Word of a duel always brought onlookers eager to view the spectacle. The news had traveled very quickly.

----Yes, I heard of the duel while at the ferry. That is why I am here.

----Please then, state yoa' business. Who ah' you?

----My name is Anna. I am to marry yoa' Stephen Pratt. I believed him to be *my* Stephen. I apparently was mistaken.

Some loud cheers welled up from the mob outside while inside Sophie stood nonplused. Hearing the noise erupt from the road, Quinton dashed to the scene. Anna broke suddenly into unrestrained sobs making her speech difficult to understand.

----I should have told you.

Her words were tainted with a gasping inflection.

----I neva' knew he meant ha'm. I just thought he wanted yoa' plantation...It neva' mattered to me, I swea', the land I mean.

The shock of it sharpened her senses. Suddenly it all made sense, and Sophie realized the extent of her error. Hopefully, it was not too late. She bolted past the still weeping Anna, through the doorway and into the boxwood alley. The crowd had become eerily silent and once again Sophie heard a loud crack emanating from the road. And this time she recognized it for what it was. A pistol shot. She grabbed the bottom of her dress and began to run in an undignified manner to the where the onlookers stood on the tips of their feet straining to achieve a better view. Her breathe was audible and her eyes strained as she reached the gasping crowd. Sophie heard a second shot.

Stephen was very pleased with the way events were playing out for him. John evidently was on to him, but for some reason it would appear he had said nothing to Sophie. It was an error in judgement trusting those vagabonds. One of them must have talked. It would not matter in just a few moments. John had played into his hand, unwittingly, and now would pay the ultimate price. These farmers sure had dull brains. They were no match for his intellect.

Stephen had sent Jack on to the road to prepare for the duel. He was not concerned in the least for his safety. He knew it was unlikely that the country bumpkin, war hero or not, would be able to pose any threat to his life using a pistol. He had not played completely by the rules of the game, of course. According to code, he was to offer, as the challenger, choice of weapons to his enemy. Men had been known to choose bowie knives on occasion. That could have been dangerous. Stephen had instructed Jack to set the distance at twenty paces. The one-armed man would not have a chance at hitting him at that range. Some fools dueled while holding the corners of a single handkerchief. That would be suicide. Nevertheless, his foe would know nothing of the rules to challenge him.

The autumn sun like a blazing eye watched from directly overhead. Stephen left the serenity of the back garden where vines of yellow jessamine wound round about a white split fence. He passed through the alley of parallel boxwoods and surprisingly to him, on to the bustle of a gathering crowd. Word had spread quickly. Folks could not resist a duel and it had probably been some time since they had seen one.

The circle of onlookers opened as Stephen stepped onto the road. Jack stood at the center of the excitement holding a silver platter in which two pistols of equal caliber resided. He looked about for his adversary. John was nowhere to be seen. A loud, hoarse voice came from just outside the assemblage of people. As Stephen looked to see what the comotion was all about he saw a tall, lanky young man in coarse looking clothes break into the open and begin shouting at him.

----Whea' is he? Whea' is the man responsible foa' the death of my brotha'? I demand satisfaction. Whea' is the one called Pratt?

----I am he. What do you want of me?

----My brotha' just minutes ago killed himself with his own gun. He said he would ratha' die than be kilt' by some fancy pants lia'! He said it'd be a disgrace!

Stephen could hardly believe his luck. He would not need to duel after all. Not that it would have been unpleasant to do so. Especially when confident of the outcome. It was a strange development for certain. One would not have thought.... he must have known I would have killed him. He stood there in his brown pants, bloused cream shirt and silk vest feeling at last like one of the planter class. He reached up and stroked the brim of his hat that covered most of his boot black hair. He tried not to show his satisfaction at the news by keeping his perfect white teeth behind his closed lips.

----I am sorry that I will not have the opportunity to prove my innocence and defend my name. He has taken that from me.

George was now pointing and shaking his finger.

----You'll have yoa' chance! I'm hea' to represent my family!

Stephen looked haughtily upon the gangly youth. If John was little threat to him, this one would be more likely to shoot *himself*. The crowd was silent waiting for a reply. Most were speechless at what they were hearing and seeing. They watched with interest as the events unfolded before them. There was a hush as Stephen poised to answer the challenge. He looked at the crowd and then at the awkward young man standing just a few feet from him. This could be tricky. To accept and kill the young teenager could bring the condemntation of the community. To refuse might be seen as cowardice. That would only reeinforce what others had been saying about him since he avoided the war. He would have to accept. But he chose his words carefully.

----I regretfully accept then.

There was no regret in him. He regretted that this would not advance him in the eyes of society, but he had no regrets about shooting the man. It was just something that had to be done. He would make it quick and painless as possible. No need for the young man to suffer. Jack, looking like one appointed to some high office, began the chain of events that would end in a duel. The choice of weapons was offered to George. He quickly chose and Stephen plucked the other from its place. Jack delivered the orders of procedure.

----I will instruct the gentlemen to stand back to back.

The assembled crowd, now realizing that shooting was indeed going to take place, spread out and distanced themselves out of harms way. The two standing before them were a comical pair if the situation were not so grave. George towered over Stephen and his arms protruded beyond his cuffed sleeves. He looked very serious and somewhat tense, but not unnerved. Conversely, Stephen stood very calm and rigid. His air was one of complete confidence and ease. Clearly, all present feared for the young man and it was evident that their sympathies lay with him. Again, a silence fell and Jack gave further instruction.

----At my signal each of you will step off ten paces on my count. When ten has been reached you may turn and fia' when ready. Truth will be decided in the test of a'ms.

The last part Stephen had never heard in any other duel, but he had added it for his own benefit. Jack concluded.

----Gentleman, ah' you ready?

Each nodded assent and Jack began to count very slowly.

----One...two....three....

Neither man looked over his shoulder, but continued to walk on, George spanning a lengthier distance with his long legs. Stephen focused on his strategy as he rythmically stepped off the paces. With novices such as this one, it is best to allow him to fire a hasty shot. He himself would stand with pistol pointed and waiting for the inevitable miss. Then he could take careful aim. He and his father had practiced this a hundred times on a stuffed uniform attached to a pole.

----four...five...six....

The silence of the gathered crowd was eerie. It was like a funeral and no one was yet dead. The monotone counting, ringing in his ears, and the empty faces all about him were beginning to creep into his focus. He must not unravel at this juncture. He must maintain his nerve.

----seven...eight...nine...

There, he was back to procedure. One more pace and let the training take over. The only threat was his wavering mind, and now it was under submission.

----ten...

Stephen wheeled expertly on his heels. In his mind he pictured the uniformed target he had struck dozens of times as a youth. And his target came into view. There the tall farmer stood with his pistol at his side apparently waiting for a first shot. The unexpected startled him, and he squeezed off a shot much sooner than he hoped, but felt it a good one. The echoes of it rose with the dust from shuffled feet. The eager spectators gawked with eyes that could be opened no wider. They stared hard at George waiting to see blood or some other evidence that the lead had found its mark. And there was. The front of the lean teenager's shirt was jagged and torn at the chest. The assemblage waited for the youth to topple or for the blood to trickle from the hole. George himself looked down calmly to the ragged cloth and reached his hand inside the tear. It was a very close call. He knew how to make himself a small target and it had saved his life. He gave himself another once-over and then being certain that he was not hit, raised his revolver and pointed it slowly and surely at Master Pratt. The long arm of his opponent seemed to reach very near to Stephen. And he was shocked. The echoes of the failed attempt were still in his ears and they became like a dirge sounding out his death. Then he remembered his adversary. Likely to miss. Still, he winced, clenched his teeth hard, and waited for the pain that he hoped would not come. First came the explosive crack to his ears. He opened up his eyes and that was when he felt the burning fire in his leg that sent him crumpling to the ground. He found the puncture in his thigh and began to squeeze to prevent the life from spilling out. He was immediately surrounded and someone tore at the pant leg and began applying a tourniquet. The crowd was now abuzz and the air filled with excited chatter. They had had good sport and noone was yet dead. Except of course for the unfortunate man who had killed himself. Honor and courage had ruled the day, and many in the crowd regretted that duelling had gone the way of the flatboat. It was just no longer useful.

John's vision was blurred as he attempted to focus. He saw green leaves swirling about in a blue haze. His head hurt and he felt like he could vomit. He was unsure where he was or what had happened. Then the world came into a sharper picture. He was beneath the walnut tree. He remembered dropping from the tree to the ground and feeling the blow to his head. John reached back and felt his scalp. There was dried and wet unkempt.   She, however, was extremely polite in returning their greeting. She then addressed George.

----Georgie, what on earth are you doin'? And wea' is yoa' brotha'?

----Well, to the first question, I'm disposin' of this dandy who picked a fight with John. Secondly, he's sleepin' quietly unda' a black walnut tree.

----Georgie, what did you do?

----I couldn't let 'im duel this Stephen fella'. John is no good with a pistol. So I gave'm a tap on the head and rode on out hea'.

----That was very thoughtful, George, but what will John say? He has built quite an honorable name for himself and yoa' family. He will feel shamed that he did not meet the challenge himself. You know how this must look.

----Oh, John'll be hoppin' mad. But I took care of his reputation. I made a scene when I got hea' tellin' everyone that I was John's second, and that he had killed himself ratha' than die at the hands of a lia'. I demanded satisfaction. It was quite a show. Yoa' friend Pratt took one look at me and figured I was easy pick'n's and agreed to the duel, all too readily I'm glad to say. You know how I am with a pistol. You can tell 'im I could have put that ball through his heart.

----But George, what will happen when they find out John is not dead?

Even as she finished the sentence, John arrived on his horse which was snorting and tossing its head about in a wild excitement. The white bib on the front of the graceful animal was flashing and its mane was flung forward as John settled him. All eyes were on the oldest Huff brother as he sat tall upon the horse just a few feet from George and Sophie. John did not even look at her, but the relief at seeing George upright gave way to his anger that he had put himself in harm's way.

----You had no right to do that, George.

----Now that ya' mention it big brotha', I think you ah' right. I apologize.

The older brother looked at the ripped shirt and realized just how close the shot must have been. He alluded to it when he spoke to his brother.

----Good thing yoa' so skinny.

John smiled vaguely, very proud of George not only for what he had done, but also for winning against a tough opponent. The crowd, still buzzing about the duel, pressed in on the trio engaged in conversation. The buzzing became laughing.

----Hey, John, we thought you was dead.

Another added.

----He sent his little brotha' to fight for him.

John was getting uneasy. Fame is often fleeting. He didn't care about the fame, but he did not wish to be regarded a coward. Not after all he had done to prove himself in the war. George shouted down the crowd.

----Take a look at the back of my brotha's head. I had to knock him out to keep him from fightin' this duel. I was a little jealous of all his war wounds, and I figured on gettin' one of my own. And this dandy wouldn't oblige me.

The crowd now laughed all the harder. It was a great story to pass along for anyone who could have been privelaged to witness the events.

----How 'bout them Huff boys. Heh, heh.

They began to pat both men on the back, laughing and having a grand time. Honor was often

Chapter Sixteen

Molly sat alone at the foot of David Croft's large, mahogany bed. She had beside her a basin of water, a sponge, and a lone candle. Just a few short years ago she had performed this same task for Misses following her untimely death. She reached in and wrung the sponge and started at the top of her gray-haired master. She gently washed back his hair and resoaked the sponge, wringing it out into the basin. The trusted servant paused before she touched it to his expressionless face. The old woman wept without restraint, tears mixed with sweat, as she leaned her turbaned head over his lifeless body. Visions of her past accompanied her careful study of his countenance.

She remembered the moment of kindness that bound them forever. She was only twelve, and he a young and handsome planter of the first class. Molly recalled that she was being taught by her previous mistress to sew, and she had not taken well to it, which caused her to be battered on many occasions. They were in Montgomery, and she had accompanied the cruel woman and her equally cruel husband to purchase Negroe cloth for the single pair of trousers issued every season to the help. While they shopped, Molly had wandered out into the street to take in the sights of the town on her first ever visit. She was standing in front of a shop where a beautiful green, satin dress was displayed. She longed to slip into the window to try it on. Just to feel pretty for one moment. In her reverie she had not seen the large overdressed woman carrying a parasol in a gloved hand. The woman began to shriek at her in indiscernible words. The young servant had failed to clear the way as the woman passed. Molly shrank back from the window as the woman continued to berate her. Her master came out at the commotion and began beating her with his walking stick. The blows were not carefully directed and Molly had suffered terrible bruises to her back, arms and legs. It was then that Marse Croft appeared on the walkway. He just stood for a moment, very near, without uttering a word until the ill-tempered man stopped the beating to acknowledge his presence. Molly looked up at him through her tears just as she now looked down upon his pleasant face. She could clearly recall the stark words for her master and even more the tender words for herself.

----It appea's this one gives you trouble.

----And what business is it of yoa's?

----I would like to make it my business, sir. I will pay handsomely foa' the girl.

----Ah, I see. Gotta a liken' foa' the young darkies do ya'?

She remembered that again, he didn't speak but that he was clearly angered and disgusted by her soon to be former master. She could read the compassion in his eyes, and she prayed silently that he would take her home. She listened to know just how much she was worth.

----I'll pay seven hundred.

----Well, she is of child bearin' age of cou'se.

----Nine hundred, and that will be my last offa'.

----Ha. She's yoa' problem now.

And he paid for her.

motioned for the girls to step forward, and where her eyes had been fixed upon her father's figure as she walked down the stairs, Louisa now turned her head aside unable to look as she drew closer. Molly put her arm around her and led her to his side, with Sophie just behind.

----Now you tell yo' daddy good-bye now, young miss.

Louisa turned to look at him and she began to cry a small, delicate cry with a slow and steady stream of tears and very little sound. Molly still had her arm about Louisa as the young girl placed her hand upon his folded hands. She leaned down, kissed his face and bade him a final farewell. Then she stepped aside allowing Sophie to draw near. Molly took Sophie's hand as she pressed close to the table where he lay.

----Its all right chil', you go ahead and cry now.

Sophie bit her lip and shook her head. She placed her hand upon his cheek for a brief moment and spoke to him.

----I know I've disappointed you, daddy, and I am sorry. Bur it's going to be all right-you will see. We will keep this place and you will have grandchildren that you will watch with delight. You will see, daddy. I love you.

And she too stepped away to rejoin Louisa. She had not noticed that the room began to fill with the sorrowful servants. One by one they began to stream past the deceased Master Croft, and each paid respects in his or her own way. One old field hand paused to speak to Sophie before he made his way out. He said just a few words that were on his heart.

----I'ze powa'ful sorry Miz Sophie. I guess it'll be time fo' me to be movin' on-I wanted ya to know. But fo' as long as I breathe, Marse Croft will be my masta'.

----That is kind of you Isaac- you have been dutiful and honest for as long as I have known you. We will find a way to manage without you.

----Thank ya' ma'am.

On and on they came and she greeted them all. Friends and neighbors began to arrive as well, and a concern began to press in on Sophie like a humid August heat. Mr. Pratt would surely show soon and protocol would dictate that Stephen be there too. She was uncertain what Mr. Pratt knew of the recent clash and a very uncomfortable encounter could well ensue. Even as she thought it, he walked through the door of the parlor. Mr. Pratt was hard to miss. He was tall and thick, but not overweight, and his hair was silver at the tips. He had a commanding presence when he entered a room, and his self-assurance was almost tangible. Sophie's eyes began to search for Stephen. She did not see him and felt reassured that he may not arrive. And that calmed her. She would liked to have known more from Anna, but that proved to be impossible. Well, it hadn't taken long to get the gist of what she had to say, anyway. How could she have been so blind to the scheme and the schemer? How much did Mr. Pratt know, she wondered. Maybe she would fill him in on the details. That might fix Stephen. She began to think about Job and her sick father and the more she thought, the angrier she became. All of it was Stephen's fault, either directly or indirectly, and she wanted him to pay. Sophie began to feel slightly guilty at her thoughts of revenge at such a sacred moment as her father's showing, but the feeling had rather overwhelmed her and rather quickly at that. She didn't feel guilty enough to stop the thoughts from streaming, however. She mused on the true story of a young woman who had been insulted by a man in town and the words had gotten back to her. She rode into town, strolled into the tavern where he was known to frequent and inquired if the words he spoke were truly spoken by him. He admitted that he had said them but that he regretted saying them. And added that there was no woman more worthy of honor than she was. The woman said, "That's all I wanted to know". She reached under her cloak, drew a revolver and shot him in the head. She was acquited for there was no man at home, save her ten year old brother to defend her honor, and as the lady telling the story to an appalled Yankee visitor stated,"What else could she do?".

Sophie entertained such thoughts and they grew in her until they felt so real that she had thought she really had carried out the deed. That was the kind of satisfaction it gave her. When she became more aware of her surroundings, she was uttering words of thanks to people automatically, sometimes looking right through them and after they passed by she had not even known what they had said. Sophie heard a buzz at the entrance to the parlor and looked out to see what was the fuss. It was John. Her heart began to race again as it had every time she had seen him of late. He had been very cold at the conclusion of the duel and she was uncertain if it was because of her or not. She was afraid that indeed she was the cause. It should not surprise her after what she had done. She had doubted him and placed his life in jeopardy, and even more, jeopardized his brother and John's honor in the whole mess. Oh yes, she was the reason for his distance. The question was, would he care enough to forgive her? Seeing him there in the doorway with so many smitten onlookers she felt a twinge of deep regret. How could she have doubted him? She determined that she would do whatever necessary to regain his trust. She was unsure how to proceed, however. There would apparently be no time for planning for he was making his way toward her. She smiled faintly as he approached; he did not smile at all.

----Sophie, I am terribly sorry to hea' of yoa' father. He was a very good man. If thea' is anything I can do, please call on me.

----You ah' very kind, John. I will.

There was a hesitation on both their parts. She knew she should say something but the words would not come. It was as if they each stood on opposite sides of a great chasm. On John's side there was barren land. On Sophie's side there were great trees that perched on the edge and if felled would easily span the distance providing easy passage. And she stood holding a saw. John looked at her waiting for her to begin cutting away. But she just stood there with that useful tool in her hand. He nodded and turned to go. Sophie watched him walk away. She was angry with herself. Why didn't she just apologize and ask his forgiveness? She suspected her pride was the obstacle and she silently cursed herself for it. She came by it honestly, though. She looked over to where her father still lay, as if to acknowledge the author of it.

Sophie was beginning to get weary. Several hours had passed since the first visitors had filed through. She had not moved from her place since the beginning and now she wished more than ever to be elsewhere. Mr. Pratt strode easily to where Sophie had confined herself for the past three hours. She gulped hard. Looking into his eyes, she saw her father and went all soft inside. She had seen them sitting or riding together so often that she associated one with the other, even more so than mentally connecting him with Stephen. His kind eyes calmed her.

----Sophie, I am so sorry. Yoa' father was my dearest friend and his oldest daughter I could not love moa' if she were my own. I promised yoa' fatha' long ago I would look afta' you when he was gone, and I am happy to honor that request. I thought it would be unda' different circumstances, howeva'.

She gasped just a little and hoped he did not notice her discomfort. He knew something. But how much? He continued a little more slowly and with greater effort.

----I know that Stephen was hurt in a duel hea'. I know what he tells me but I am afraid that he has been dishonest with me. I am awa'e that it is not the first time. One does not like to think on such matta's, but at times it is unavoidable. He tells me he challenged a man that he did not name foa' impugning oua' family honor and foa' insulting you, Sophie. I fea' no number of duels could possibly repai' the damage done by him to oua' good family name. I am certain he has shamed us in the matta' but I am uncertain just how. I fea' I will know soon, and be faced with the consequences of it. If it is as I believe, I apologize in advance foa' my son. I must bare some of the responsibility myself in guarding him too ca'efully and in giving him too much. It is a grievous burden to carry, the disgrace of a good name. It is equally difficult to imagine a beloved son acting dishonorably to a trusted friend. Can you tell me I am wrong , Sophie?

Sophie lowered her eyes in affirmation. She could not tell him--- she could not. When she looked up again she could see the pain in is face and it gripped her already strangled heart. Ironically, it was she who forced some words of comfort.

----He wishes only to please you. He has been misguided in his efforts but his desia' is always to make you proud. He will need you now very much. I am afraid his ambitions hea' have been dashed to pieces. I hope you can find it in yoa' heart to help him pick them up no matter what he has done. He is still yoa' son and he can yet make you proud.

----So it is true then. I dare not to guess what he has done. I regret most that I will not have you as my daughter, Sophie. Yoa' fatha' had every reason to be proud of you. I wish it were me thea' in that box ratha' than David. I would ratha' be gone than to suffa' the disgrace of a peevish, self-centered child who would offend my dearest friend.

----Oh, Mr Pratt, Stephen has done nothing that cannot be foa'given. Please, go and talk to him and I am certain he will divulge the whole matta' to you. It is not my place to set the events befoa' you since Stephen knows them fa' betta' than I.

She felt tremendous pity for him and it eased some of her own pain to have a twinge of empathy for another. She secretly hoped that Stephen would lie to his father again rather than place upon him the disgrace of his treachery. She should not have trivialized Stephen's sins, but she could not watch Mr. Pratt shrivel before her any more than he had. He hugged her affectionately and joined the others for the processional that was due at any moment. The room cleared and

Molly came to lead the girls away. Sadie was just behind her dressed in white with a white turban piled high upon her head. Molly was in identical garb. In perfect contrast, Sophie and Louisa were adorned in black from head to foot. They lowered their gossamer veils and went out. Six dark African women dressed in white were followed by the black shrouded box and the white faced friends and family all dressed in black. They were in turn trailed by the family servants that escorted the remains of David Croft to his final resting place.

Molly returned to a house steeped in silence. A pall rested upon the Croft home that seemed would never clear. The old slave retired to her quarters, exhausted and deeply concerned for the future of Croft plantation. She had overheard many of the hands talking of leaving for other opportunities. Molly had pressed upon them to stay, but they seemed determined. She dropped into her bed and closed her eyes. She could still see the face of Master Croft behind her lids and she uttered a prayer on his behalf. She prayed that God might be as kind a master to Marse Croft as he had been to her. Then she dozed into a deep and restful sleep.

Chapter Seventeen

The days and nights since John had last seen Sophie on that now familiar stretch of road that bears the Croft name had passed ever so slowly. The harvest season had gone well, and the corn shucking party was as fun as John remembered it being when he thought of them at war. The family and servants had divided sides and the corn lay in two big piles of even numbers. John was the leader of one group and his father the general of the other. The signal was given and the excited participants shrieked and laughed as they tore the husks off the ripened corn. The competition broke the monotony of husking and was a long-standing tradition in many families. John, seeing his troops faltering rallied them to an increased frenzy but it was to no avail, and his delighted father was able to claim victory. There were no losers, however, for all feasted to satisfaction that day and enjoyed themselves completely well into the night.

As much as John had cherished those memorable days, a sense of yearning came over him that was as natural as the need to eat. He was becoming restless, and the days that had passed, along with some deep introspection, gave him some answers. Sitting still allowed him to recognize there was something missing in his life. As much as he wished to think of himself as one who needed no one, or no thing, he was quite empty without someone to share his existence. He had the daily example of his father and mother to remind him of all that he was missing. Their greatest sense of joy was in each other and in their children. It might have been easier had he not found someone specifically that he wished to share himself with. And so he thought very much about going to Mississippi where some of his kin had gone. He could start over there and maybe escape this neediness that clung to him. And as long as Sophie ws near, he would not be able to shake her memory. There was the other option. He could go to Sophie and reestablish their relationship. Even in his most thoughtful moments, seated on a stump by a white oak fire, he could not figure why this option was not a viable one for him. George had talked to Sophie and she knew what had happened with Stephen and the assaults. Yet she made no attempt to see him. And so he would not go to her. As the months passed it seemed less likely that he would. After the corn shucking there was the hog killing. Season was giving way to season and he found himself sinking deeper into isolation. It was like that first kiss. The further away from it he got the more he doubted its reality. His affection for Sophie was becoming like a very pleasant dream that he wished not to wake up from. For when he did awake there would be the inevitable yearning.

It was December and the cheer that always accompanies Christmas Day would surely chase away the demons that could in no way survive the spirit of the season. John sat staring out the window into the night on this eve of Christ's birth. It was much colder than usual and the draft that squirted through the window casement made the candle on the sill, flicker. He turned from the window to take in the beauty of the festive decorations. The small tree sat on the large wooden table in the dining area. It's boughs were weighted down with clusters of nuts and fruit. Long strings of popcorn circumscribed the shapely tree. Stuffed dolls, tenderly sewn by Susan graced the branches and colorful pieces of glass reflected the jittery candlelight and what little sunlight was left that streamed through the openings in the room. It was a wondrous sight, and the plebeian Christmas scents poked their delicate fingers into every corner of the room. Heavy pine, cinnamon, apple, and vanilla tobacco burning from father's favorite brier delighted the senses. The little ones were giddy with excitement, and John could do nothing but smile. Certainly, these were the best things in life. He was suddenly aware of Susan, her cheeks ruddy and her teeth white.

----John, are you just going to sit thea' and smile? Come join the rest of us. We won't make you sing, I promise.

She reached for his hand, and they walked side by side to where the others had gathered to sing carols. Before Susan let go of his hand she turned to him quickly as if she had forgotten something very important.

----Oh, John, I had almost foa'gotten. I was by Sophie's the other day and invited her to spend some of Christmas Eve with us. She should be hea' within the half hour. Did she mention it to you?

----Now, Susan, you know I haven't spoken to Sophie since August.

----It occurs to me that you haven't. What was I eva' thinkin'? You might just go splat yoa' hair down a bit. It is stickin' up every which way. Oh, and Louisa is comin' too. It seems oua' little brotha' has taken a fancy to her.

----It is a shame that I can not be hea'. I need to gatha' moa' wood and tend to the animals. Wish them both a Good Christmas foa' me.

John hurried up the stairs. Susan frowned as he turned abruptly to go and so did Edna who was eavesdropping.

He looked at his own image in the glass and wondered what it was that Sophie ever saw in him. From appearances it wasn't his dashing good looks. Stephen was certainly better to look at. Even he recognized that. And Stephen was whole. John figured there was something in him that Sophie evidently liked, and it was reassuring to know that it was more than just his shell. But it had been so long since they had spoken, he wondered if she still did like him.

John cupped his hand with water and dumped it on his recalcitrant cowlick. It did not respond as he had hoped. The hairs sprang back with great resilience. He figured it didn't matter much and let it go. Just another part of the shell. His last thoughts before he parted with his, what he believed to be substandard reflection, were of his actions regarding Sophie over the last four months or so. He really wasn't angry with her and his affection for her had not dwindled in the least. Maybe it was the shock of seeing her standing there with her hand in Stephen's just after she had agreed that they could spend more time together. Oh, and the fact that she consented to marry Stephen might have something to do with it. But it wasn't anger that he felt. In all of his thoughtfulness those nights by a slow burning fire, he had never carried the source of his feelings this far. Maybe because of where it led. He was hurt. Pure and simple, she rejected him. And it hurt. It was easier to avoid than to address. Well now, that felt better. What to do with it was the next thing. The "why" of it he could chase forever. He would have to leave that to Sophie.

For himself, he had to decide whether to fight or quit. And up until now he had quit. And that was unlike him. Struggling with himself was harder than fighting the Yankees. He loved her and it was time he started acting like it. He thought of Warren as he turned to go back to where the singing was. He thought of Warren's parting words to Julia and the choice between love or honor. He had fought honorably and returned home a proud soldier who had endured the rigors of battle. He would live to have his fight for love. Maybe Warren was wrong. One could have them both. Love. As quickly as one can become a hero or a coward he had become a man in love. He would not have believed it could happen so quickly. He would tell her. Today. This Christmas Eve,1865.

With resolution John climbed down the ladder and joined the others. His father was sitting by the fireplace cluttered with stockings telling stories of Christmas past. Georgia Anne was in his lap looking very concerned. She had found out over the last couple years what it meant for Santa that the North and South were engaged in bloody conflict. As it was explained to the then three year old, Santa couldn't get through the Yankee blockade. It was the family's way of telling her there wouldn't be much under the tree for her that year. She had taken it very well, counting it her sacrifice for the war effort. Everyone felt a little bad that they allowed her to heap all of her anger on the Yankees. That couldn't be good for her. Even if they *were* to blame for the scant Christmases.

Melissa, now eight years old, sat near her father's feet. John looked at her flannel gown and dangling pig-tails. She was fair-boned and fair-skinned.

Secretly, she was his favorite. She had been from his earliest memories of her, quiet and inquisitive and she adored her older brother who seemed more like her than Warren did. She had written him a few Christmases ago asking if he would "make the Yankees leave Santa go" so that the family might have Christmas. "But," she added, "Please don't get hurt". He had shared the letter with his comrades who were so moved they looked to have been ready to blaze a trail for Ole' Saint Nick at that very moment. He wrote back that they were doin' their best but the Yankees had gotten very stubborn and would not let him pass. It was the time of his greatest longing for home, Christmas. And on this Christmas he didn't fail to be thankful that he was back in beautiful Alabama, and back in his home. He closed his eyes for just one moment and offered up a heartfelt thanks for his home, for his life, and for his family. He experienced in the brief moment of prayer satisfaction so great that he felt he might burst from the fullness of it. A familiar voice, melodic and sweet, prompted him to open his eyes to the soft yellow light.

----Hello, John. Merry Christmas.

He looked up to see Sophie standing over him. She was aglow from the angular pulses of the fire. John was so taken by her he felt he had been ushered from his prayer directly to heaven and had been greeted by an angel of the highest order-something like a present day Elijah. He had never seen her look so beautiful. And then he realized that it was just that way every time he saw her. He recognized it as a very good thing. Her dress was cream colored with traces of ivy dotted by delicate white flowers. It tapered to fit snugly at her waist which looked no bigger 'round than a fence post.

It then blossomed to the floor in a perfectly proportioned drop. Sometimes the dresses stayed too narrow at the bottom and looked very unflattering. Other times they expanded rapidly and excessively which was more unsightly. But she was just perfect. John rose to his feet and greeted her properly.

----Merry Christmas to you, Sophie.

He took her slender hand in his and kissed it formally.

----Did you bring Louisa?

----I did. But I fea' she has found William and we will not be seeing her again foa' some time.

----I hope he hasn't taken her back to fatha's cookery, if you know what I mean. Maybe I should just peek in on 'em.

----I will go with you....that is....if you don't mind.

Could he have been more obvious. He wanted to just tell her, "Of course. That is why I said it. Do you really think I am concerned they are in the whiskey?" But he chose different words.

----Shua', that would be nice. I would like to hea' how you have been since I last saw you- with yoa' fatha' gone and all. *Nice? That would be nice?*

Sometimes it really bothered him that he seldom said things as he wished to. Maybe he should just speak how he felt more often and quit fishing for the right words. It wouldn't be *nice*. He *needed* to talk to her. He had important things to say.

They walked out into the dusk, past the black walnut trees silhouetted against a blue-gray sky. He felt the eyes of his brothers and sisters, the well-wishers, as he escorted her out. He could hear the whispers begin before he even shut the door. Now they were alone gliding down the pathway to the spring. And he was fidgety. He was afraid the words would come out all wrong and he would lose his chance once and for all. He wasn't even sure how to begin. She began for him.

----I have heard from Mrs. Humes who is a very close friend of Mrs.Clay-the forma' senata's wife. She says thea' is hope that her husband is to be released from prison soon. It is a tragedy how they have treated the man. No one, North oa' South doubts his innocence.

This was safe. He relaxed a bit.

----That is welcome news. We have lost too many good men to this fight. Do they really believe Clement Clay was a conspirata' to Lincoln's death? I heard some say it would be moa' likely foa' General Lee to be accused of duplicity.

----The poa' man's been through a terrible ordeal. They have locked him up with no charges whatsoevea'. They talk about treason and conspiracy but they have nothing. My friend tells me this Judge Holt, who is a very avaricious man, has a grudge against Mista Clay and has found a way to settle it.

----I am certain thea' will be no end to those stories. It will be much like oua' revolution against the British. The winna's will retrieve their own form of justice from the defeated and site the fo'tunes of war as good reason.

----And the injustices stretch to the women and children also. Mrs. Clay has been stripped of her clothing and searched for illegal documents of all things. A'my officials have searched her bags and confiscated personel possessions. She has not been allowed to even see her husband until now, and it took a visit to President Johnson to get it done.

----I imagine President and Mrs. Davis are not faring much better with his imprisonment. Oa', I should say fo'ma' President Davis.

----So I have heard. He is locked in a cell and they tried to put him in shackles. That is when his easy nature was ova'come with rage. I have neva' heard of the man so much as raising his voice.

----Next, Thomas Nast will have him on the cova' of *Harper's Weekly* cursin' and throwin' punches at an innocent jaila'.

----So I assume you have seen this Christmas issue? Can you believe the audacity of them having the heads of oua' beloved generals lying at the feet of an ova'sized figure of U.S Grant "The Giant Killer"? Very insensitive. I would like to have a word oa' two with Mista' Nast.

----Shua', and then the next thing you know you'll be a featured cova'. I imagine he would have you in a tattered dress with one hand holdin' a heavy chain and a dozen negroes at the end. You would have a Confederate battle flag draped ova' yoa' shoulda' and yoa' free hand would be balled up and waggin' at a cowerin' Grant.

----Why John, I think you have a hidden talent, although I'm not shua' I like yoa' representation of me.

They laughed aloud as they passed the spring house and the chicken coops and barn. They continued to walk into the open, narrowing fields that led into the wooded hollow and the distilleries. White smoke could be seen rising from a handful of them up ahead. After the light laughter faded, Sophie spoke with a softened voice.

----I guess I can't blame you foa' whateva' picture you have fo'med of me.

They now stopped and faced each other. Sophie's head was bent low, and John searched for her eyes so that he might read her better. He was learned in the ways of women enough, although far from knowledgeable, he believed, to know that one could read the eyes better than to hear the words, because sometimes the words betrayed the true feelings. He would have to count on the words because she would not look at him. She went on.

----I put you in a terrible spot and foa' that I am very sorry. I doubted yoa' intentions and I ruined a chance foa' us by accepting a proposal from a man I didn't love. Foa' that I am ashamed. I don't want to excuse my actions, but I do want you to understand why I agreed to marry Stephen. It was fea' really---a terrible fea'.

She now looked up into John's inquiring eyes. She continued.

----Jack Arp came to me with a wild story about you tryin' to get oua' prope'ty and it was very compelling. He said he saw you standin' ova' the last of the men that assaulted me and that you questioned him and then let him die. I was afraid I had allowed my feelings to cloud my judgment. I don't know what happened and I don't care to know, now. I know whateva' happened was no plot against me, and John, I should have known that then. So I figured if I could not have someone in my life to love, I would look to taking care of my family and home at whateva' the cost. That is why I agreed to marry Stephen. I was wrong.

----Wrong in taking care foa' yoa' loved ones and yoa' home?

----Wrong in thinking that it could replace loving you.

----I'm a little slow sometimes, Sophie. What ah' you tellin' me?

----I love you John. And I hope that you can foa'give me. But if you can't I'll understand.

And so here was his chance. He was a little afraid to say anything other than, "Of course I forgive you", but he thought he might risk saying how he felt, even if he might mess it up with the wrong words. He would put his faith in the honest truth giving it that same high place as love and honor. Its virtue could rise above a foolish word or a misspoken thought. And so he plunged into the breech with great courage.

----Of cou'se I foa'give you, Sophie.

And then he froze. He lost sight of his plan of attack as simple as it was. He started to search for the right words as she looked hard at him obviously wondering how her love, set before him on a platter might be received. It was like the first cooked meal of a new wife. He had taken the first bite as she watched and waited. And he had waited too long in response for her to believe it when he said it was "delicious". She took a step back when he said no more, formalizing the conversation. John sensed he was loosing his opportunity with her and blurted out.

----Let's have dinna' togetha'.

It was all he could think of with the analogy of a meal running around in his brain.

----That would be fine, John. You ah' very gracious.

He was losing her. He had made it seem that an apology was all that he could deliver. She had handed her love on a platter and he had pushed it back to her. It was not too late. He rallied, remembering the course he had planned to take. Forget everything else and tell her straight.

----No, wait, Sophie. It's not dinna'. It's not just a walk oa' a visit oa' a carriage ride. That man who I was standing ova', wounded, tried to kill me and I shot him. I had to know who it was that was tryin' to hurt you. I made him tell befoa' I would help him. He told me Stephen put them up to the assault and befoa' I could help him, he died. Jack must have figured somethin' else. I wasn't sure if maybe he was part of it, so I kept the information to myself until I knew things foa' shua'. I planned on bein' with you a lot to make shua' you were safe, and then I happened upon you and Stephen. It was too much to see. Then afta' the duel and all, I let my pride and hurt get in the way of seein' ya' like I wanted to all along. I was beginnin' to think I would end up my life loving no one at all, Sophie. And then thea' was you.

He looked deep into her hypnotic eyes and spilled it all out without groping for words. He just told her how it was. And then he concluded, finishing what he knew was the oratory of his life.

----And the sum of it is, Sophie, I love you too. And foa' as long as I live I will love no otha'. Those aren't just words. Time will bare me out.

She had moved closer with each word and now she was pressing in ever so near to him. John cupped his hand to the small of her back gently drawing her even closer. And for only the second time. He kissed her. This time it was more familiar, intimate. There was no tension or awkwardness. It was a perfect moment. One that could be rendered among the finest memories in any life. And certainly the sweetest in his.

----John Huff, I do believe you have foa'given me. You could neva' kiss me like that if you hadn't. And so what do we do now?

----Let's meet on yoa' front piazza and discuss it tomorrow.

----You want to spend Christmas Day togetha'?

----I had almost foa'gotten, but, yes.

----John Huff, how could you foa'get Christmas?

----It must have been the kiss. I'll probably think of nothing else 'till the next one. So tomorrow then?

----Ok, John. I must tell you, though. If you intend on kissing me again, you'll have to marry me.

----So noted.

His face beamed and he chuckled lightly. She asked,

---- Shall we walk a little furtha' and see if we find the young ones?

Sophie slipped her arm through John's and they walked deeper into the hollow. William and Louisa were not to be found there among the smoking distilleries, so John and Sophie returned to the house arm in arm.

Chapter Eighteen

Since the death of his employer things had improved steadily for Jack Arp. Sophie had turned much of the plantation matters over to him as she immersed herself in the education of her sister. She had even insisted that he move into her old room after she had taken her father's. Of course there were the difficulties. The plantation was still in heavy debt and would continue to be with the failure of the '65 crop. Add that the servants were leaving to explore their new found freedom and the economics of Croft plantation were looking even more bleak. The carpetbaggers were still showing up at the door and offering ridiculous prices for the land. They never failed to mention the delinquent taxes. Still, he was content. Since the duel he was rather famous. Everyone wanted to know the story of the fight and what his involvement was. The rumors had become outrageous. It had gotten back to him that he had kicked up dust on the road to cover the underdog in a protective cloud, thus obscuring the view of Stephen to take a good shot. It was absurd, but he didn't bother to deny it. And there was more. The good citizens had heard he had moved in with Sophie Croft. In spite of the circumstances it was an exciting time for a thirty-year-old overseer. He was living the life of a planter. Stephen Pratt had tried and failed. Yet he, Jack Thomas Arp, in spite of his humble upbringing--the son of a Scot-Irish farmer and a Cherokee bride--had elevated himself through thrift and hard work to the house of a planter. His children would be shown deference and respect. And when giving advice on matters of law, ethics or economics, his voice would be one heard above the masses.

Jack Arp had no foresight. All around him was the evidence of crumbling. The foundation on which he had built his dreams was eroded. Only a fool could have missed the signs. But maybe he had seen them and refused to let go of the dream. Plantation life was over. The ways, values, and customs of the Old South were caked on the bottom of Sherman's boots with the Southern soil, and when he reached the ocean and washed them in the Georgia tide, the Old South was washed away with the dirt. Croft plantation was down and would not recover. The relationship between master and beloved family servant was changed forever to be replaced by mutual suspicion, and often downright hatred. The gap between planter class and yeoman had blurred with the Mason-Dixon line until there was little to separate the two. The South, like the planter, had fallen far.

Yet, Jack Arp continued walking the railroad track he was on, not seeing the speeding train that was just ahead. His life was improving as he saw it, and the best part of it was Sophie. And here too, he let himself be misled. He spent minutes, days, hours, in her close proximity. He was glad she had not found him out--that his careful watch of her was not at all at her father's request. It was of his own volition that he concerned himself with the small matters of her life. He had designated himself her sole protector, her guardian, and had *earned* the right to call her his own. He had secretly escorted her to parties; he had hunted and killed her enemies; he had followed her, out of sight, as she walked alone in the darkness on evening strolls. His care for her was unlike Stephen's who had only his lust driven desires for power as basis for his claim. Many nights he had watched her through darkened windows, sitting straight backed at the piano, or stepping gracefully across the shining wooden floors of the blood-red parlor. And now the house in which he was only occasionally a guest had become his home. And the girl he watched from windows was his partner.

He believed Sophie recognized his affection, too. They had grown close over the last three months. They breakfasted together in the mornings and rode the boundaries of their lands on tepid evenings. And so he believed it was time. It was only natural they should be joined. It was the next step. A short step. And after all she needed him. For all practical matters they were living as a couple. That is what he would propose to her, and he felt she would assent. It all made sense. He would be beside her forever, watching over her--taking care. Her overseer.

Sadie passed by the large oak table in the pale yellow dining room where Jack was sitting, screwing up the courage to plead his case to Sophie. He barked at her. She turned and looked at him with obvious contempt. He was not liked by the help.

----Sadie, whea' is yoa' misses?

A light of obvious relish oozed through the antipathy. She was going to enjoy this. Sadie was very aware of the overseers infatuation with Sophie.

----Now le'see. She went a visitin' wif missah Huff. Thas' right. She took Miss Louisa, too.

The tightening of his face could be seen even through the sparse beard. Sadie followed up.

----Mussa' been some pa'ty or sumpin' cuz' she wuz' all gussid up.

Jack turned back to the window to hide what was already very evident. He was visibly upset. He could see in the reflection of the glass the greenery that garnished the windows and the pine roping that entwined the staircase. He sipped his coffee and began to think on the significance of Sophie's visit. She was not through with John Huff. This was not the kind of Christmas he had hoped for. And all was going so well. Jack's concentration was interrupted by the sound of neighing horses. Sophie had returned. He saw in the reflection of the window the door open and the two lady Crofts enter. Only Sophie approached. Louisa went upstairs. Jack remained silent, facing the window. She called out his name.

----Why Jack, why ah you lookin' so thoughtful on this Christmas Eve.

----Just thinkin' 'bout all I have to be grateful foa'. I didn't know you was goin' out.

----I didn't decide until late.

He finally turned to face her.

----You shua' look fine, Sophie. Did you have a pa'ty?

----I was invited to the Huffs. I know you ah' cautious about John, but we had a chance to speak and I have all confidence that he is both honest and sincea'.

----Those ah' kind things to say 'bout a man. Sounds if you kinda' like 'im.

----I do, Jack, very much. I love him and I told him so just tonight.

She watched the air go out of Jack Thomas Arp, yet she was completely ignorant of the cause of it. She fumbled along the wrong course.

----Oh, I know you ah' still suspicious of him, Jack. You have been such a dea' watching out foa' us since Papa died, and I am grateful. I promise, yoa' position hea' is secua' and nothing need change just because John and I will be spending time togetha' again. He will gain yoa' trust if you will let him. Just wait and see.

He pressed his lips together and forced a smile to hide the distress. But he could not speak.

----Come now, Jack, it is Christmas Eve. Be in high spirits, will you? John will be hea' tomorrow at nine to celebrate with us. You of cou'se will be a gentleman, I'm shua'. It will be a wonde'ful day.

----Nothin' else would do.

----Now that's betta'

----If you'll excuse me I've got a matta' to see to. I'll be back within the houa'.

----But on Christmas Eve?

----Necessary business, Ma'am.

He hadn't called her ma'am in some time. He slipped away quickly, was on his horse and gone in a matter of minutes. He rode in the darkness toward Leesburg. It was there he would find help for the idea that was forming in his head. For all the maneuvering of the gentleman and the hero it was he who was poised to take the prize. One more deft move and she would be his. But he would need Stephens's help. He knew where to find him. Stephen had slipped into despondency since the wound he suffered in the duel. He had been shunned by his father and it caused him to turn to the demon alcohol for comfort. He had been spending his days and nights in a tavern in Leesburg. And even on this Eve of the savior's birth, he knew where Stephen would be. And together they would form an unholy alliance on this holy night. It was a short ride to town and Jack had arrived more quickly than he would have thought. His mind had been turning since he left to attend to the mental details that would make his plan fool-proof. Jack hitched his horse and stepped into the unusually quiet drinking, gambling place. It was empty but for one lone soul whose dark head was flat upon the table. He showed no sign of life. There was an empty bottle in one of his hands. Jack stepped cautiously to where he lay, silent. He kicked the chair the man was on and the head of the slumbering gentleman turned lethargically to face him. It was a handsome head even though the hair was quite mussed.

----Pratt?

----Yeah, who's askin'?

----It's Jack Arp

----Who?

----Jack Arp. I was the oversea' at Croft Plantation.

----What do you want with me? Can't ya see I'm busy?

Jack pulled up a chair and straddled it backwards across from Stephen.

----Ya' look pretty low.

----If you are hear to trouble me, may I suggest you go somewhere else. You have picked the wrong night.

His voice and manner were threatening and Jack thought it good the man was in an agitated state.

----Whose fault is it you ah' hea' in this place?

Stephen glared at the overseer, saw the squinted eyes and inferred that the small-statured man before him was here for a purpose.

----Go on.

----I know what you want and I can make it happen. But we will have to act quickly. Which would be sweeta' foa' you---revenge oa' Croft Plantation.

----Umm. A tough choice. I'm listenin'

----I currently run the prope'ty.

The dandy let out a short laugh which angered the overseer, but he maintained his course. The message in the laugh was obvious. Jack ignored it.

----I will sell out to you at a price you will no doubt appreciate. Sophie will have no knowledge of the buya'. I will make her believe the land can not be saved.

----And what of the revenge.

----A chance to even the scoa' with John Huff.

----And what do you get in all of this?

Jack Arp did not answer. He remained stone-faced waiting to continue with the plan. Again, Stephen Pratt raised his voice in derisive laughter, and again the overseer ignored him.

----I see. So the lovely Miss Croft has yet another admirer.

----Are you interested or not?

----What do I need to do?

----Yoa' war hero is coming to see Sophie tomorrow at nine a.m. I will see to it that he show up at the Croft cemetery at that time. The whole family and the servants will be at the house foa' Christmas. It's tradition. I'll also arrange that one be missing. You'll shoot John with this gun. It came from the old man's collection. Leave it by his side and get out. Thea' will be a grave partially dug with a shovel. You'll not be suspected. The shot will be my signal to come, so get out in a hurry.

----A startled grave robbin' nigga'. I like it.

----John's "circle" friends, myself and Sheriff Weed, will take care of justice befoa' anyone can eva' talk. When I hea' yoa' shots I will be the first to arrive--- A witness to the crime.

----Sounds too good. Very little risk. Very high prize. I'm in.

----Good. I will meet you hea' two weeks from today.

----So that's it?

----That's it.

----And I am to trust you?

The plotter nodded and turned to go. Stephen Pratt leaned back in his chair and raised the bottle high in salute to the exiting overseer turned partner. Jack Arp mounted his horse and began his ride back through the chilling night air that promised rain.

Chapter Nineteen

Each falling drop of rain was a harbinger of the danger that lurked on this Christmas morn. And although the falling water only dampened the spirits of the inhabitants of Croft Plantation, had they known the course that was set for this day they surely would have wished for another. As it was, Christmas was brighter and more cheery than the last few in spite of the rain. It was half past eight o' clock and as was usual, the children, both black and white, filled the house with their laughter. They came bounding into Sophie's room looking for their stockings. It brought to her memory the same scene of last Christmas. The children burst into her room, exultant, full of childish wonder. The economics of war had created a dire situation, and there were no gifts for the young ones. She could remember the saddened faces; the broken hearts that nearly broke her own. The poor children who had suffered right along with those who had made this war. They were innocent. They knew nothing of states' rights. They just wanted Christmas back. It was then that she hated what the war had wrought. And yet she could not abandon her love for the cause since so many had spilled their blood to advance it. She held several of the teary-eyed negroe children close to her and they all wept together. They mourned for Christmas and longed for the Christmases of old. In her troubled spirit she searched her mind for solace in theWord. She remembered the tears of the children of Israel as they gazed at the new temple after their return from Babylonian captivity. The older men and women wept tears of sorrow at the sight of it because they remembered the grandeur of the previous temple. What made Christmas of late so difficult was the grandeur of those past.

But this year was different. The blockade and the war were both ended and Sophie had managed a few trinkets for the children of the plantation. She rose and led them down the stairs and to the tree where the remaining servants waited, gifts in hand, for the "missus" of the house. She stood beside the decorated tree looking for Jack. He was not to be found. Everyone else seemed to be present with the exception of Silas, the stable hand, who she guessed was still tending to the horses. Sophie welcomed them all, the happy faces that were so familiar to her. They brought their gifts and laid them before her with a warm Christmas greeting. Quinton entered the room smiling, carrying the stockings filled with gifts for the children. He carried also, gifts for the servants. There were colorful turbans he passed out to all the ladies, much to their delight. And to all the male servants she gave plugs of tobacco and new socks. It was a very happy Christmas for all. In the midst of the jubilation Sophie stood pensively for a moment feeling very pleased with the joy that surrounded her. And her thoughts turned to her father. It was her first Christmas without him. He always enjoyed this day very much. And she was always warmed by his generosity on the occasion. She missed him and her mother profoundly. A small tear slipped down her cheek as she thought on it, and then she turned to wondering where Jack might be and when John would arrive. He should be on any moment. It was nine o' clock.

Jack Arp waited a little way out the Croft Ferry Road. And just as he predicted, John Huff was very punctual. It was five minutes to the hour and the chestnut horse with the white bib sloshed down the muddy road toward him. John slowed and reined in next to him.

----Merry Christmas.

He was pleasant but formal. He was still a little wary of the overseer, but couldn't quite figure why. Jack was nervous, jittery---his mouth twitched as he spoke.

----I just came from Sophie. She asked that you meet her at her fatha's grave site. She's waitin' now. This path'll take ya directly thea'.

He sniffed, wiped his nose on his sleeve. He spit tobacco on the soft red mud. John hesitated, feeling that something wasn't quite right. He attributed it to his uneasiness with Jack in general and decided to press ahead to the cemetery. She probably wanted him there for support, this being her first Christmas without her father. He nodded and touched his hat to the slight man on the ragged horse. And he prompted his own to gallop onto the wooded path. It was quiet and the rain had turned to nothing more than a drizzle that could not reach him through the thick of trees. He slowed as he neared the clearing that was the Croft burial place. John felt an intangible hint of dread as he came full into the open. His eyes were constantly moving, searching for some sign of danger. Sophie was not at her father's still fresh-looking grave site. As he neared, he saw that it had been disturbed. There was overturned earth and a shovel thrown on top and the quiet around him gave evidence that she was not on her way. It just didn't feel right. Even as he was thinking it, a familiar, distinctive "click" alarmed him. He sat upright on the horse, unmoving, waiting for the next sound--- the echo of gunfire from somewhere behind him. But there was nothing. Then, a low deep voice.

----Good monin' massah Huff. I'z gots a k'ismas gif' fo' ya'. Yuz' can turn 'roun'.

John turned slowly on his horse, very uncertain as to what might appear before his eyes. To his astonishment, Stephen Pratt stood with his arms at his side. Behind him was the servant Silas with something metal in his hand that looked like a gun. It wasn't. It was a horseshoe. Stephen must have thought the cold metal on his neck was a pistol. It was a peculiar sight---the large, black servant clad in wool and muslin standing behind the dandy, Stephen, with a horseshoe held to his head. A gun was on the ground at Pratt's feet. It wasn't difficult to ascertain what was happening. He had been set up.

----He'z amin' t' shoot ya' missah Huff. 'Dat Jack Arp sent me 'dis monin' t' check 'da catches on 'da pine trees fo' 'da terp'tine. I stopped t'pay my res'pecs to marse Croft on 'da way when I saw 'dis verm'n in d'brush. 'Da sounds of yo' horse drown out my steps 'n I jus' walk right up on 'm.

----Well done, Silas.

Stephen Pratt just glared at him. He was disheveled in his fine clothes. He was wrinkled and

219

smudged, and his eyes were red and swollen. His black
hair swept across his forehead and rested on his brow.

----What'll I do wif' 'im missah' Huff?

Pratt could hold his tongue no longer and so
began spewing his invective.

----Well now what to do. First, you send your brother to
do the fighting and now you leave it to a negroe. Do
you ever do your own fighting hero boy? How did you
really lose that arm?

----Take that ho'seshoe from his head, Silas.

Stephen turned a contorted, angry face to the
large servant and sneered, realizing he had been duped.
John dismounted the horse and stood just five paces
from his adversary. The dandy scoffed.

----So, you are going to fight. Should I tie one arm
down? You know, to make it even.

----I wouldn't recommend it. You'll need both of 'em.

Stephen rushed upon him, but John side-stepped
causing him to tumble away from him, arms and feet
flying. Before Pratt could rise, the veteran landed a
forceful kick to the thin ribs of the would be assailant.
He rolled over with a gasp for air, then nimbly jumped
to his feet, still hunching from the well placed blow.
Finding himself near the senior Croft's grave and the
planted shovel, Stephen picked it up and moved
menacingly toward John. Silas started to step in and
was waved away. Pratt swung the tool at John's head,
missing, but sending him sprawling to the ground. He
dropped the shovel and leaped upon his foe, straddling
him and pinning John's one good arm with both of his.
He quickly reached behind his back and drew forth a
large bowie knife. John was unable to move. Stephen

laughed fiendishly as his victim languished on the ground beneath him. The knife was placed to his throat.
----Your going to die on my property. And your lady friend will marry an overseer.

Stephen was relishing in the victory, his white teeth flashing. Silas, visibly disturbed, again approached. Stephen checked his advance with a warning.
----I wouldn't do that. You see, when I kill hero boy hear there will be two stories---yours and mine. Now, who are they gonna' believe? And if Mister Huff here and I are both dead, Ole' Jack will track you down in a day. I'll make you a deal. You take that horse and go. I'll make sure Jack doesn't look too hard for you. Start yourself a new life somewhere.

Silas stood for a moment taking it all in. He realized the truth of what the other spoke and recognized the predicament he was in. He began to walk slowly to where the horse was, just opposite him. The muscular stable-hand began to circle around the place where the helpless John lay beneath the sneering, triumphant Stephen Pratt. As he made his way to the mode of his escape, he stopped suddenly and looking down saw the gun that had been in Stephen's hand. He reached and picked it up, turning to face the onlooking Pratt. John had stopped struggling for the moment, the bowie knife being pressed too sharply to his throat. He could feel the warm blood trickle down the side of his neck, the blade having been applied with just enough pressure to break the skin. He was waiting and praying for some opportunity to free himself. He wanted to call out to Silas to help, seeing as how they were both going to die anyhow. But he knew the docile nature of the African

221

and in spite of Silas's obvious physical power, it was unlikely he would fight. He, like the rest of his race, had been subject to the power of whites for too long. And silent obedience was the norm. So it was to his great surprise and delight the conversation that ensued.

----What are you doing, boy? Think, you ignorant savage. I am giving you a chance to live.

----I may not be 'smart as you, but I do knowz' if I run they'll be no livin' no how. So if'in two've us dies, 'din three dies.

And he raised the gun.

----Put the gun down or I'll cut his throat, I swear.

Silas pulled back the hammer. John, aware possibly of his last chance, swung his leg in a quick sweep, landing the heel of his boot on Stephen's head striking him in the temple and sending him toppling to the ground. Both men were quickly to their feet. Stephen was still holding the knife and was poised to throw himself again at John. He looked to finish the deed he had started. Before he could pounce, Silas made his presence known.

----Step out da' way, Marse Huff. I'll shoot 'im, shur' 'nuf.

Stephen had little choice. He cursed aloud, jumped on the chestnut horse, and sped away but not before Silas touched off a misplaced shot in his direction as he fled.

----That was some quick thinkin', Silas. I thought I was done foa'

----Meanin' no disrespec' sih, but ya' shoulda' let me take care'v 'im when I could.

----Now Silas, what were you goin' to do, shoe him?

----Now dat's 'muzin missah' Huff.

When the laughter had cleared, John spoke more seriously.

----You know Silas, Jack Arp set you up.

----Ya', I done figur'd 'dat out.

----Had the plan worked, I would be lyin' hea' dead and you would be arrivin' about now after hearin' the shot. They set that shovel to make you look like a grave robbah', and me bein' the one who surprised you hea'.

John examined the gun Silas was holding. A name was etched in the handle.

----Mista' Croft's gun. Yep. You were good and set up.

----Whats we do now?

The muffled sounds of horses' hooves on soft earth reached their ears. They would have to decide quickly. It was Jack Arp riding alone.

----Give me the gun, Silas. You run on and tell Sophie what just happened. Tell her to stay put and that I'll be on presently. If you hea' shots you keep right on goin'. If anything happens to me, tell Sophie to go to Sheriff Weed. He can be trusted. And don't delay. If he kills me, he'll be afta' you next.

----Ok missah' Huff. I shua' hope'n 'dat you knowz what youz' doin'.

Silas darted off on a circuitous route through the woods, carefully making his way back to the plantation home. John picked up his slouch hat that had fallen during the scuffle and stood staring in the direction of the nearing horse and rider. The drizzle was gone but the air was still thick with potential rain. Jack's gaunt face and narrow frame came into sharper focus as he rode to the place where John stood. The overseer slowed, eyes barely visible beneath the brim of his hat. There was no warm Christmas greeting. John sensed that this man was not so glad to see him, alive anyway. The grim overseer spoke first.

----I heard shots. What happened?

John decided the direct approach might just be best-- dispense with the games.

----Sorry to say, Jack, but yoa' plan did not work out like ya' hoped. Although it was very clevah'.

----I don't know what yoa' talkin' about.

----Shua' ya' do, Jack. Stephen and I just had a little talk.

The overseer began to work the tobacco in his mouth more vigorously with the words. He was clearly rattled. He reached slowly for the Colt revolver that was thrust into his belt.

----Don't botha', Jack. I've got this nice revolva', that I believe belonged to Mista' Croft.

----Whatta' you want from me?

----Now, thea' a question. I want you to leave. Leave hea' and neva' come back.

John could see him turning it all over in his head, weighing his options very quickly. His nostrils were flared and his teeth were clinched. A question was coming and John expected it.

----What if I choose to stay?

----You wouldn't want to when Sophie finds out what you've done.

----What if she neva' finds out.

----You mean if I die hea'?

No answer.

----I thought of that. Silas, the one you tried to set up, is telling Sophie the whole story right about now. They'll be a posse lookin' for ya' two days from now, unless of cou'se you just disappea', and we'll forget this whole murder conspiracy thing,

Jack sat for a moment deliberating the whole deal. When he reached a decision he asked another question.

----Can I get some of my possessions back at the house?

----They'll be delivered to the ferry landing at noon tomorrow. Someone will be waitin' thea'.

Jack, with a violent rush, wheeled the horse and sped away and out of sight. John Huff breathed a sigh and gave a brief prayer of thanks for his safety. He looked up to the gray sky and providence, and wondered when the giver of all good things might see fit to order his life in a more docile path. He started onto the narrow lane that led to the plantation house. He began to massage the aching shoulder of his lifeless arm. The unwelcome activity brought with it the relentless pain. He passed the corn crib, the stables, and the whitewashed slave quarters that were empty. He neared the back piazza and was greeted with a rush of movement. Sophie burst through the door, hurried to him, and threw her arms around his neck.

----Oh John, I was so afraid! Silas told me what happened. How could I have been so mistaken?

----You see the good in everyone, Sophie. That's one of the things I love most about you. And, Merry Christmas by the way.

She put her head to his chest and he cradled her close. John looked down at the soft brown ringlets resting on the fabric of the green silk she wore, the only silk dress she kept after she had donated the others to the now defunct army. She smelled of lavender and the silk was smooth to his touch. He put his head down to further feel the silky smoothness of her skin on his cheek, but when she raised her soft eyes to him he saw that she was again crying very small tears. He spoke tenderly to her.

----Sophie, I have seen you hu't and I have seen you cry. And quite honestly it pains me.

But the wo'st of it would be if I were not the one to hold you and tell you it will be betta'.

Thea' is only one way foa' me to be shua' of that, Sophie---that I will always be the one to wipe yoa' tea's.

He reached his hand to her face and with a simple gesture stroked her cheek. She looked long into his blue eyes trying to determine if what she believed was happening, really was. Instead of uttering the words she expected to hear, he for only the third time cupped her face and kissed her. John withdrew and just looked at her, expectantly. He spoke not a word, but rather waited as if it was she who was to speak. As she did not respond, he led her to understanding.

----Ah' you a woman of yoa' word, Sophie Croft?

She was even more confused, but answered, nonetheless.

----I have always followed the example of my parents who have taught me to speak truthfully in all matters, and to honor my word as I do my good name.

----You said a few months ago that you owed me yoa' life. You said yesterday that if I kissed you again we would have to marry. I am asking foa' you to keep yoa' word, Sophie, and I fully intend to see that you honor it. Will you give me yoa' life. I will return it in even better condition. Will you marry me, Sophie?

----John Huff, you certainly wax eloquent on big occassions. I will keep my word, not because I am honor bound to do so, but because thea' is nothing greata' I aspia' to be than yoa' wife. I will marry you.

Again they embraced, and again Sophie began to cry. Only this time they were tears of joy. John did not bother to sweep them from her face.. These tears brought a smile to his own.. Aunt Molly opened the door to the back piazza chattering something about getting things moving and something about food being ready. She stopped abruptly when she realized she had interrupted a private moment. She winked at John, knowing by instinct what had occurred, and pulled her head back inside the door.

It didn't take Sophie long to begin thinking on the practical matters of a wedding.

----Oh, but when, John? I have so much to do!

For all the reflection about love and marriage he had engaged in, he had not ventured into the realm of time. He had not given it one thought. So, of course, he was at a loss to respond. But unlike his earlier botched attempts at eloquence, this time he remained calm. He was learning what to say, and what not to say to those of the opposite sex.

----When is yoa' motha's birthday?

He could see in her face that he had responded well. She looked at him and he could almost hear the words he thought she must be thinking."What a thoughtful gesture." Then she screwed up her face.

----It was just last week.

----Ummm. Yoa' fatha's?

She brightened.

----In May.

----Shall we make it then?

----Oh yes, yes. I have so much to do! What a wonde'ful Christmas this is.

Sophie hugged John once more, affectionately, and turned to go into the house. Out of the corner of her vision she could see the rustling of the curtains in the back window. Six dark faces with pressed noses quickly withdrew. What began as an inauspicious day ended as fortuitous as either family could remember.

Chapter Twenty

For the last five months God had smiled on Croft Plantation. It was May 17th, the weather had been good, and the steady stream of defecting servants had trickled to a halt. The latter was in large part because of John's influence. Since the hasty departure of Jack, John had come to live at Croft plantation. The help took to him far better than they did the unpredictable and often temperamental former overseer. John worked in the fields with them as he had done at his own home. The more underclass farmers did not have the luxury of having the servants do all the work. In fact, the Huffs hired day laborers to help them farm the land. The three servants the family had were usually disposed with house matters or child care.

And so on this May 17th the sun shone brightly and the birds sang more cheerily than on most spring days. The flowers were more vibrant and the sounds of laughter more pervasive. It was the day of John and Sophie's wedding, and it seemed that God, knowing the struggle which had been theirs, saw fit in his infinite kindness to bless them with the most lovely day of the year. The ceremony was to take place at the front of the plantation. The boxwood alley would serve as the aisle she would walk to meet John. The servants had spread a white runner and boughs of laurel down the last forty feet of the alley. Sunlight in spots broke through and dotted the tapestry like large white flakes of fallen snow. The end of the alley opened to the gallery of seats that would hold the well-wishers. The runner extended up the stairs of the piazza where a makeshift altar, also draped in white, had been set with the implements of the Lord's Supper. The face of the plantation with the columns, altar, runner and white lattice, shone brilliantly in the early afternoon sun. The lattice that ran beneath the piazza was entwined in yellow jasmine that filled the air with the most delectable scent that heaven could offer as a wedding gift. Nowhere had anyone ever seen a more fitting place for a sacred ceremony.

John had spent the evening at his home and was preparing for the coming nuptials. He peered into the same looking glass that just that winter had returned a disappointing reflection. He looked happier and healthier, he thought. He was a golden brown in color and he wore the gray uniform of his service, with some alteration and repairs of course. Sophie had insisted he wear it and he did not resist, feeling it would be the most appropriate garment he could wear. John looked down from the glass to the top of the wardrobe and saw two wrapped objects resting in the same positions they had occupied for some months. The one was partially undone that held the severed arrowhead which was Warren's. He regretted that his older brother could not be present for the event. His oldest brother would surely have been the first by his side. Warren no doubt would have made some smart remarks about "marryin' up". In fact, he would have had good sport with the whole relationship. John reached in his one pocket and pulled the locket given him by George that had the silk ribbon and Sophie's picture attached. He put it back in, reached to the top of the wardrobe, and unwrapped the arrowhead. He took it in his hand and remembered Warren's words that night by the fire. John had battled for honor and for love and his life was now very full as a result. He decided then and there that he would live every day fulfilling Warren's dream, and never forget the opportunity he had been given to pursue it. He clutched the token once in his hand and with some sentimentality thrust it in his other pocket. There was one neatly tied package left on the wardrobe. It was his own keepsake that he had left unwrapped until now. With care, he untied the bow deftly, using his working hand. He unfolded the corners and reached inside with thumb and index finger, then withdrew a small circle of gold that had on it a mounted diamond, small but brilliant. He regarded it as something very precious, indeed. It was his grandmother's wedding ring that had been given to his father, and who in turn had given it to Warren when he learned of his coming marriage. Warren, just days before they left for their respective fates at the hands of the Gods of war, had turned it over to John. He had said then, that he didn't believe he would return, and had asked that John give it to his own girl when the time came. John had tried to laugh it off and called him a sentimental fool. But it troubled him nonetheless.

With watery eyes, he slipped the ring into his shirt pocket where it would be accessible. George strode into the room grinning from ear to ear.

----Look at you, Johnny boy. They fixed that ol' rag up nice. Repaired those holes and everything. The marriage of Johnny Reb. I like it.

----Sophie insisted. She said she always wanted to marry a sold'iah.

----As if they don't know already.

George paused a moment, then asked,

----' Ya scared? They'll be a bunch folks thea'

----Thanks for remindin' me. No, I'm all right.

----You shua' you want to do this? 'Cause I'll fill in if ya' like.

They both had a good laugh and departed together for Croft plantation.

----Now Miss Sophie, Yuz gots to sit still or I'll stick that pretty face a yoa's.

----I simply can't sit still, Molly. I am a bride to be this day and the last thing I care to do is sit.

----Yu' neva' cared for the stuff 'dat gals do growin' up no matta' how I trieds to teach ya'. Nows ya' payin' fo' it.

Sophie too sat before a glass that she had been displeased with for reminding her of the bronze skin she wished that she could have whitewashed like the servants quarters. And very rare for her sex, she was actually pleased with her appearance that she found acceptable on this her wedding day. And well she should. She was the very picture of loveliness. Her dress was simple but elegant. The ballooned sleeves gathered at her upper arms and the neck rounded out to the ends of her shoulders. Her hair was pinned back in a swirling bun and sprigs of delicate jasmine and orange blossoms traversed her hairline just before the pinned veil that descended below the base of her neck. Sadie and Molly finished their fussing and urged her out. The violins were playing and the time had come.

----Le's go now Sophie, youz don't wanna' be late foa' yo' own weddn' now.

They slipped out the back of the house and wound their way quickly to a break in the alley without being seen by any of the guests. Molly and Sadie took again to straightening and fussing as Sophie stood ready for her call to appear. Louisa was already standing and ready, her role being first. She was accompanied by George who gave Sophie a nod to reassure her that she was indeed presentable to be a bride.

The music began again to signal Louisa and George to enter the alley and proceed to the altar. They stepped lively and took their places on either side. There was again a pause and Sophie could hear but not see the gallery stand, and the music struck again the bridal call. Sophie stepped into the sun-spotted alley and she could see John there waiting. She could remember their walk together that first day almost a year ago, and she felt certain that John in that moment was thinking on it, too. She began her rhythmic steps to the altar with Aunt Molly in a white turban close behind. She could see out the sides of her vision the smiling friends and servants that had gathered. But she never took her eyes off John. She halted just at the bottom of the steps and Molly stepped in beside. The minister began the ceremony.

----Who here gives this women to this man?

Molly spoke softly in reply.

----At 'da request of her daddy, I do.

She smiled and sat as Sophie, with the help of George, stepped up before the minister and the altar John greeted her and took her arm in his. She listened carefully as the clergyman read from the Word of God, the chapter of love. "Love is patient, love is kind" and the words she heard most clearly for it seemed very fitting for their relationship, " love bears all things, hopes all things, endures all things." He then looked up to them both and quoted, "Love never fails".

He instructed them to face each other and explained the significance of exchanging rings. The circle is symbolic of eternity. Its path is never ending. And so forever the two of their lives would be entwined in a union that could not be broken.

Sophie looked deeply into John's eyes that were even more blue as they absorbed the sunlight that broached the shade of nearby trees. She knew that he would be the only man she would ever love, and she could see beyond the blue windows as she looked through them to the inner man, that he reserved all his devotion for her. He pulled the ring from his pocket and placed it on her finger. Louisa handed a ring to Sophie and she did the same. He pronounced them man and wife and as the first act of marriage the two then knelt at the altar and recieved communion. When they had finished the Sacrament, the divine bade them to stand and face the well-wishers. Sophie looked out over the assemblage and felt the warmth of love from family and friends that reached to her like an ocean wave lapping at her feet. And it was even more refreshing. The clouds that seemed to hover over the plantation had scattered and all that remained was this perfect day and this perfect moment where she stood before God and men and she was recognized by both as Mrs. John Huff.

The couple descended the stairs and greeted those who had shared in their celebration. When they had thanked nearly everyone, John took Sophie by the arm and led her once again into the boxwood alley.

----You said you had a su'prise foa' me, John. Whea' ah' you taking me?

----Whea' takin' a little trip, Sophie.

She could see as she neared the end of the alley that Tobias was waiting with the carriage. When they arrived, John helped her aboard and they started down Croft Ferry Road.

----John, the only thing ahead is the rivah'.

----You ah' right, Sophie. Tobias must be goin' the wrong way.

She noticed that in spite of it, John made no effort to turn him around.

----So we ah' going to the rivah'?

----It seems so.

----My dea' husband, what ah' you up to?

He just turned to her and smiled. When they arrived at the Coosa River, Tobias wished them well and helped them disembark. They were alone at the ferry landing, and as a final act before he departed, Tobias dropped a large carpet bag on the ground beside them.

----Is this a long trip, John?

She was looking at the bag.

----I had Molly pack a few things foa' you.

----So it really is a trip.

John walked over to where the stock of wood was left for the steamboats and picked up a torch and lit it. Sophie was beginning to understand.

----We ah' takin' a ride on the steamboat? To whea', John?

----We ah' not riding Sophie. We ah' goin' to run.

They laughed aloud together, remembering their childhood prank with Warren. Then Sophie got serious.

----You don't mean it do you, John?

The Laura Moore came chugging up the river and John signaled her stop. This time they did not run, but boarded and walked to the upper deck. They were greeted by a waiter who still showed the signs of a severe burn, but who was cheerful nonetheless.

----It is good to see you again Mista'. Huff. It would appea' that all has worked out well foa' you.

----It has indeed.

He escorted them to a table in the first class. When he seated them he said, "With my compliments. I hope you have an enjoyable stay in Montgomery." Sophie was obviously pleased with the surprise. John reached across the table and took her hand in his. That afternoon they had their first of many dinners together as husband and wife, and they spoke of the children that they hoped would some day be theirs. John thought on his good name that he now shared with his wife. He also thought on the honor he hoped it would bring to his offspring. And Sophie thought on the love that filled her heart. It was a love that she hoped her own children might someday know.